"Not every st
sight."

"No," said Joss, her face suddenly shadowed. "Outside of fiction very few, probably." She braced herself, nerving herself up for confrontation. Showtime. No point in dragging it out. "Is one of those glasses for me?" she asked, and moved forward into the light to take one.

Dan took an incredulous look at her and dropped one of the glasses on the stone flags.

There was a deafening silence.

"What's known as a *pregnant* pause," said Joss at last, deliberately flippant.

Catherine George

THE BABY CLAIM

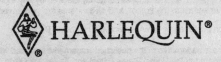

HARLEQUIN®

TORONTO • NEW YORK • LONDON
AMSTERDAM • PARIS • SYDNEY • HAMBURG
STOCKHOLM • ATHENS • TOKYO • MILAN • MADRID
PRAGUE • WARSAW • BUDAPEST • AUCKLAND

ISBN 0-373-12148-2

THE BABY CLAIM

First North American Publication 2000.

Copyright © 1999 by Catherine George.

All rights reserved. Except for use in any review, the reproduction or utilization of this work in whole or in part in any form by any electronic, mechanical or other means, now known or hereafter invented, including xerography, photocopying and recording, or in any information storage or retrieval system, is forbidden without the written permission of the publisher, Harlequin Enterprises Limited, 225 Duncan Mill Road, Don Mills, Ontario, Canada M3B 3K9.

All characters in this book have no existence outside the imagination of the author and have no relation whatsoever to anyone bearing the same name or names. They are not even distantly inspired by any individual known or unknown to the author, and all incidents are pure invention.

This edition published by arrangement with Harlequin Books S.A.

® and TM are trademarks of the publisher. Trademarks indicated with ® are registered in the United States Patent and Trademark Office, the Canadian Trade Marks Office and in other countries.

Visit us at www.eHarlequin.com

Printed in U.S.A.

CHAPTER ONE

WHEN she was certain the balcony was empty Joscelyn Hunter hid behind one of its pillars and let her smiling mask slip. For what seemed like hours she'd laughed and chatted and circulated like the perfect guest. But enough was enough. It had been a test to come to the party alone tonight. But Anna was her oldest friend. Missing her engagement celebrations had never been an option.

The breeze was cool, and Joss shivered as it found her bare arms. Soon she could make some excuse and go— where? Home to the empty flat? She stared malevolently at the view, lost in angry reverie, until at last a slight cough alerted her to unwanted company. Joss turned with bad grace, to see a tall man with a glass in either hand.

'I watched you steal away.' The stranger held out one of the glasses. 'Something told me you might be glad of this.'

Because there was no way she could snap at one of Anna's guests and tell him to get lost, Joss muttered perfunctory thanks and accepted the drink.

'Would you rather I left you to your solitude?' said the man, after a long silence.

Joss looked up into his face. A long way up, which was a novelty. 'You've as much right to look at Hyde Park as me,' she said, shrugging.

'I'll take that as a no.' He touched his glass to hers. 'What shall we drink to?'

'The happy pair?'

He echoed her toast, but barely tasted his wine.

'You don't care for champagne?' she asked politely.

'No. Do you?'

She shook her head. 'Secretly I detest the stuff.'

'Your secret's safe with me,' he assured her.

Joss relaxed against the pillar, surprised to find she rather welcomed the man's company after all. It was certainly preferable to her own. 'Are you one of Hugh's friends?'

'No.' He shrugged rangy shoulders. 'I'm a friend of a friend. Who dragged me along.'

She looked him up and down, amused. 'You're a bit on the large side to be dragged anywhere. Why were you unwilling?'

'I'm no party animal. But the friend disapproves of my social life. Or lack of it.' He leaned comfortably on the other side of the pillar. 'All work and no play is bad for me, he tells me. With monotonous frequency. So once in a while I give in and let him have his way. Don't drink that if you'd rather not,' he added.

'I've been on mineral water so far. Maybe a dose of champagne will improve my mood.' She drank the wine down like medicine.

Her companion nodded slowly. 'I see.'

She tilted her head to look at him. 'You see what, exactly?'

'I've been watching you for some time. Noting your body language.'

She stared up at him in mock alarm. 'What did it say?'

'That something's not right with your world.'

'So you came charging to my aid with medicinal champagne.' She shook her head in pretend admiration. 'Do you often play Good Samaritan?'

'No. Never.'

'Then why now?'

He leaned closer. 'Various reasons. But mainly because I'm—curious.'

'About what, in particular?'

'The mood behind the smiles.'

'I'd hoped I was concealing that,' Joss said gruffly, and turned away to stare across the park.

'No one else noticed,' he assured her.

'I hope you're right. The last thing Anna needs is a spectre at the feast.'

'Anna's a friend of yours?'

'Oldest and closest. But too euphoric tonight to notice anything amiss.'

Her large companion moved until his dark sleeve brushed her arm, and to her astonishment Joss felt a flicker of reaction, as though he'd actually touched her.

'Do you live with Anna?' he asked.

'No, I don't,' she said flatly, and shivered.

'You're cold,' he said quickly. 'Perhaps you should go in.'

'Not yet. But you go, if you want.'

'Do you want me to?'

'Not if you'd prefer to stay,' she said indifferently, but hoped he would. In the dim light all she could make out was the man's impressive height, topped by a strong-featured face under thick dark hair. But what she could see she liked very much.

'Take this.' He shrugged out of his jacket and draped it round her shoulders, enveloping her in a warm aura of healthy male spiked with spice and citrus. 'Otherwise you might get pneumonia in that dress,' he said, his voice a tone deeper.

Joss gave a laugh rendered slightly breathless by the intimacy of the gesture. 'You don't approve of my dress?'

'No.'

'Why not?'

'If you were mine I wouldn't let you out in it.'

Joss gave him a sub-zero stare. 'Really!'

'I'm not famous for tact,' he said, lips twitching. 'You asked a question and I answered it.'

'True,' she acknowledged, and thawed a little. 'The dress was very expensive, in honour of the occasion. I like it.'

'So do I!'

The dress was an ankle-length tube of black crêpe de Chine, edged with lace at the hem and across the breasts, held up by fragile straps and side-slit to the knee. Joss looked down at herself, then shot an amused look at her companion. 'But you don't approve?'

'No.'

'And I was so sure I looked good in it,' she said with mock regret.

'Every man present thinks you look sensational,' he assured her.

'Except you.'

'*Especially* me. But it's a very ambiguous dress.'

Joss found she was enjoying herself. 'A strange word to describe a frock.'

His deep-throated chuckle vibrated right through the fine bespoke suiting, sending a trickle of reaction down her bare spine.

'It may be a party dress to you,' he went on, 'but to me it smacks of the bedroom.'

Her chin lifted. 'I assure you it's not a nightgown. I don't sleep in this kind of thing.'

'Which makes me even more curious about what you do—or don't—sleep in,' he said softly, sending a second trickle down her spine to join the first.

'We shouldn't be having this conversation,' she said brusquely.

'Why?'

'We've never met before.'

'Then let's introduce ourselves.' He took her hand in a hard, warm clasp. 'Tell me your name.'

Joss stared down at their hands, amazed to find herself flustered by his touch. 'Let's not get into names,' she said, after a moment. 'I don't want to be me tonight. Just call me—Eve.'

'Then I'll be Adam.' He shook her hand formally. 'The party's almost over. Take pity on a lonely stranger, Miss Eve, and have supper with me.'

Joss gave him a very straight look. 'I thought you came with a friend.'

'I did. He won't mind.' He bent his head to look in her eyes. 'What was your original plan for the evening?'

Joss turned back to the view. 'Originally I did have a date for tonight,' she admitted shortly. 'But it fell through. Which accounts for the lack of party spirit. Consequently—Adam—I don't much fancy bright lights and a restaurant.'

'Then I'll get a meal sent up to my room here,' he said promptly, and grinned at the incensed look she shot at him. 'All I offer—and expect—is dinner, Eve.'

'If I say yes to a meal in your room,' she said bluntly, 'you might expect a lot more than that.'

'I was watching you long before you vanished out here,' he reminded her. 'I know you're not the archetypal party girl out for a good time.'

'Do you?' Joss detached her hand and gave him his jacket. 'But you have the advantage, Adam. If you watched me earlier you obviously know what I look like. I haven't even seen your face properly yet.'

He shrugged into his jacket, then moved to the centre of the balcony. From the room inside a shaft of light fell on a strong face with an aquiline nose and a wide, firmly clenched mouth. His cheekbones were high, the eyes slanted, one heavy dark eyebrow raised towards his thick, springing hair as he bore her scrutiny.

'Well?' he said dryly. 'Will I pass?'

With flying colours, she decided. 'All right—Adam. I'd like to have supper with you,' she said quickly, before she could change her mind. 'But *not* in your room.'

He smiled wryly. 'Then tell me which restaurant you prefer and I'll arrange it.'

Just like that. Joss eyed him curiously, in no doubt that if this man asked for a table no restaurant, however sought after, would refuse him. She thought it over for a moment, then gave him a straight look. 'As you've gathered, I'm not in party mood. But we could have supper at my place—if you like.'

His lips twitched. 'Can you cook?'

'I offered supper, not haute cuisine,' she retorted.

He laughed, then moved into her shadowy corner to take her hand. 'I'm delighted to accept your invitation, Miss Eve.'

The charge of electricity from his touch hinted at danger she chose to ignore in her present reckless mood. 'Let's go, then,' Joss said briskly. 'But not together. You first.'

He nodded. 'Allow a discreet interval for me to thank your friends. I'll have the car waiting at the main entrance in twenty minutes.'

When she was alone Joss leaned on the balcony for a while, almost convinced she'd imagined the encounter. But a furtive peep through the curtains showed her new acquaintance dominating the group clustered round Anna and Hugh. Very nice indeed, thought Joss, reassured, and much too tall to be a figment of anyone's imagination. She waited until he'd gone, then emerged from her hiding place and joined Anna and Hugh.

'We were about to send a search party for you, Joss,' said Anna indignantly. 'Where on earth have you been?'

'Communing with nature on a discreet balcony,' said Joss demurely.

'Alone?' asked Hugh, grinning.

'Of course not.' She batted her eyelashes at him. 'Anyway, must dash—supper for two awaits. Thanks for a lovely party. See you soon.' Joss hugged Anna, kissed Hugh's cheek, then did the rounds, saying her goodbyes, made a detour to tidy herself up in a cloakroom, and at last took the lift down to the foyer, where a man in hotel livery ushered her outside to a waiting car.

'You're late,' growled an impatient voice as she slid into the passenger seat.

'Sorry. Couldn't get away.' Joss gave him her address with sudden reluctance, hoping this wasn't a colossal mistake.

'I'd begun to think you'd changed your mind,' said Adam as he drove away.

He was very nearly right. 'If so I would have sent a message,' she said crisply.

'Ah. A woman of principle!'

'I try to be.' Joss turned a long look on the forceful profile, and saw the wide mouth twist a little.

'I hear you, Eve, loud and clear.'

'Good. What happened to the friend, by the way?'

'When told I was dining with a ravishing lady he sent me on my way with his blessing.'

Joss laughed. 'You're obviously very *old* friends.'

'We've known each other all our lives.'

'Like Anna and me.' She sighed. 'I just hope Hugh makes her happy.'

'Is there any reason why he shouldn't?'

'None that I know of. I like him very much.'

'Then it's marriage itself you distrust?'

'Not exactly. But Anna is so certain they'll live happily ever after. And all too often people don't.'

'Leave your friend to her quite obviously besotted fiancé and concentrate on yourself, Eve.'

'Thanks for the advice,' she said tartly, and made polite small talk until they arrived at a modern apartment building sitting in surprising harmony with its Victorian Notting Hill neighbours.

Adam parked the car, then followed Joss into one of the lifts in the rather stark, functional foyer.

'I live on the sixth floor,' she said, feeling a definite qualm as the door closed to pen her in the small space with her large escort.

Adam frowned down at her. 'You're not comfortable with this, are you?'

'Not entirely,' she admitted.

He shrugged. 'In which case I'll just see you safely to your door and fade into the night.'

Joss felt sudden remorse. 'Certainly not,' she said firmly. 'I invited you to supper so I'll provide it.' She looked at him questioningly. 'Would you really have left me at my door?'

'If you'd wanted that, yes. But with great reluctance.' He pressed her hand in reassurance. 'I keep my word, Eve.'

'If I didn't believe that I wouldn't have invited you here,' she assured him.

Inside the flat, Joss led her visitor past her closed bedroom door and switched on lights as she took him along a narrow hall into a sitting room with tall windows looking out over communal gardens. The room was large, with free-standing shelves crammed with books, and a pair of brass lamps perched precariously on the top shelf. Otherwise there was only a small sofa and a large floor cushion.

'Please sit down,' said Joss. Half empty or not, the room looked a lot smaller than usual with her visitor standing like a lighthouse in the middle of it. 'Supper's no problem because I did some shopping today. But I wasn't expecting company so all I can offer you in the way of a drink is red wine—or possibly some whisky.'

'Wine sounds good.' Adam let himself down on the sofa, and stretched out his endless legs. 'If it's red it should breathe, so I'll wait until the meal. Can I help?'

Joss shook her head, chuckling. 'No room for giants in my kitchen. I'll open the wine first, then throw a meal together. Shan't be long.'

As she worked swiftly Joss decided she liked the look of her unexpected guest very much. Not handsome, exactly, but the navy blue eyes, dark hair and chiselled features appealed to her strongly. So did the air of confidence he wore as casually as his Savile Row suit. She tossed a green salad with oil and vinegar, carved a cold roast chicken, sliced and buttered an entire small loaf, and put a hunk of cheese on a plate. She shared the chicken salad between two dinner plates on a forty-sixty basis, put them on a tray with silver, napkins and glasses, added the bread, cheese and wine, and a bowl of fruit, then went back to the sitting room and put the tray on the floor.

Her guest swung round from his absorption in her bookshelves to smile at her. 'A wide range of literature,' he commented.

'My main extravagance. Do sit down again.' She smiled in apology as she poured the wine. 'I'm afraid it's a picnic. You may live to regret not having your hotel dinner.'

'I doubt it.' Adam received his plate with approval. 'What could possibly be better than this?' He looked up, the indigo eyes holding hers. 'Thank you, Eve.'

'My pleasure,' she said lightly, then curled up on the floor cushion to eat her own meal, realising this was the truth. After resigning herself to a solitary evening, probably not even bothering to eat at all, the present circumstances were a vast improvement.

'For me,' said Adam, raising his glass to her in toast, 'it's a pleasure—and a privilege—I never anticipated when I first set eyes on you tonight.'

'When was that?'

'The moment I arrived. You stood out from the crowd.'

'Because I'm tall,' said Joss, resigned. 'But how on earth did I come to miss someone of your dimensions?'

'We were late. And it was the hair I noticed, not your height. You had your back to me, but you were facing a mirror. I could see that narrow face of yours framed in it, and wondered why the eyes were at such odds with the smiling mouth. The contradiction intrigued me.'

'I'm glad I didn't know,' said Joss with feeling. 'Rather like being caught on Candid Camera. I hope I was behaving myself?'

'Of course you were. The perfect guest.' Adam helped himself to more bread. 'But I could tell you weren't in party mood. I was surprised—and impressed—that you stuck it out so long.'

'So you saw me disappear,' said Joss thoughtfully.

He nodded. 'At which point inspiration struck. At worst, I reasoned, you would send me packing.'

'And at best?'

'The privilege of talking to you.' He gave her a direct look. 'My imagination never got as far as this.'

'Chicken salad and questionable claret?' she said flippantly.

'Exactly. Now, tell me why you asked me back here tonight.'

Joss shot him a warning look. 'Certainly not to share my bed.'

'I thought we'd sorted that out already,' he said impatiently. 'Listen to me, Eve. In basic terms, I swear I won't leap on you the moment we've finished supper, or at any other time—is that blunt enough for you?'

Blunt and very reassuring, decided Joss. 'Yes. Thank you.'

He eyed her searchingly. 'You've obviously had bad experiences in the past in this kind of situation?'

She shook her head. 'I never invite men here for supper.' Which was true enough.

He frowned. 'Never?'

'Never.'

'Then why me?'

'Because you were in the right place at the right time,' she said candidly. 'I was in need of company tonight, and you offered yours.'

Adam leaned forward, one of the heavy brows raised. 'You mean I happened to be nearest, that any man would have done?'

'Certainly not,' she snapped, and jumped up. 'You were kind. I liked that. But, best of all, you're *very* tall.'

He looked amused. 'Is height a vital requirement?'

'No. But for me it's a definite plan. I'm five feet ten, with a passion for high heels.'

Adam laughed as he refilled their glasses, and took very little persuading to finish off the bread and cheese. She offered him the fruit bowl. 'Have one of these to go with it.'

His lips twitched as he took a shiny red apple. 'Very appropriate, Eve. Will my life change for ever after one taste?'

'Try it and see.' Joss smiled and sank down to her cushion again as his strong white teeth crunched into the apple. 'Sorry there wasn't any pudding.'

'This is all a man could ask for. Company included,' he added. 'Do you feel better now?'

'Yes. I haven't been eating well lately.'

'I didn't mean the food.'

'I know. And since you ask, yes, I do feel better.'

'Good.' Adam finished everything on his plate and put it on the tray. 'Shall I take this out to your kitchen for you?'

She shook her head. 'Leave it. I'll see to it later.'

'Much later.' He looked at her steadily. 'I've no intention of leaving yet.'

Joss was glad of it. The last thing she wanted right now was solitude.

'I've respected the veto on names,' he went on, 'but is it against the rules to ask what you do with your life?'

Joss decided against telling him she was a journalist. That might give too much away. For tonight she would just be romantic, mysterious Eve. 'I'm—in publishing.'

'Fiction?'

'No. Fact.' Joss settled herself more comfortably. 'How about you?'

'Construction.'

Joss was struck by a mental picture of suntanned muscles and heavy loads of bricks. 'It obviously pays,' she commented, eyeing his clothes.

'If you mean the suit,' he said, straight-faced. 'It's the one I keep for parties and funerals. My Sunday best.'

'Is it really?'

'Absolutely.' His eyes roved over her tawny blonde bob, the wide-spaced eyes, the faint suggestion of tilt to the nose. His gaze lingered for a moment on the full curves of her mouth, then continued down until it reached her black silk pumps. 'I don't think you bought any of that in a chainstore, either.'

'True. I felt Anna's engagement party deserved something special.' Her eyes clouded. 'And when I bought it I was in belligerent mood.'

'Is this something to do with the dinner date that fell through?'

Joss smiled bleakly. 'In a way.'

'But there's a lot more.'

'Oh, yes.' Her eyes glittered angrily. 'A whole lot more.'

'Would it help to tell me about it?'

Joss frowned, taken aback.

'It's easier to confide in strangers,' he pointed out.

'I see. I confide my pathetic little story, you offer me a shoulder to cry on, then off you go into the night and we never meet again?' She smiled. 'I think I saw the movie.'

'I'd prefer to alter the script a little,' he said, chuckling. 'But whatever you tell me will be in strictest confidence.'

'Like confessing to a priest?'

Adam shook his head. 'Wrong casting.'

She nodded, looking at him objectively. 'You're right. You don't suit the role.'

'But I'm a superb listener,' he assured her.

'And you're curious?'

'Interested, certainly.'

Joss gazed at him for a moment, weakening by the second in her need to talk to someone. Anna would have been her normal choice, but that, like staying away from the engagement party, had been out of the question. At least until Anna's celebrations were over and the new, yawning gap in Joscelyn Hunter's life could no longer be hidden.

'Are you sure about this?' she asked.

Adam nodded decisively. 'I want to know what was behind the Oscar-winning performance tonight.'

Joss gave him a wry little smile and took the plunge. 'I used to share this flat with my fiancé. A few weeks ago he walked out on me.'

CHAPTER TWO

Joss had made an all-out effort to get home early for once. She'd rushed through the door, laden down with groceries for a celebration dinner. And almost fallen over the luggage in the hall.

As she'd stared Peter Sadler had rushed from the bedroom, his face the picture of guilt. 'You're home early!' he accused.

Joss nodded coolly. 'And you're obviously not pleased to see me. Is there a problem?'

'Yes, you could say that.' He took the grocery bag from her. 'I'll put this in the kitchen. Would you like some tea?'

Joss stood tense with foreboding, watching as Peter filled a kettle and put teabags in a pot. 'So what *is* the problem? And why the suitcases? Are you going somewhere for the firm?'

'No.' He turned to look at her, a truculent look on his fair, good-looking face. 'I've resigned.'

She stared incredulously. '*Resigned? Why?*'

'I got in first, before they could fire me.'

Joss shook her head in disbelief. 'This is terribly sudden, Peter! If you were that worried they'd fire you why didn't you talk to me about it?'

'When?' he threw at her in sudden anger. 'You're never here.'

'That's an exaggeration,' she snapped. 'We share a bed, remember? You could have given me a hint on one of the rare occasions you stayed awake long enough to say goodnight.'

'You know I need my sleep,' he said sullenly. 'And lately there's been precious little to stay awake for. We haven't made love for weeks. You lust for your job more than you ever did for me.'

Joss felt as though her entire world was disintegrating. 'You've obviously been building up to this for a long time. I've been blind.' She thrust an unsteady hand through her hair. 'I know you've been very quiet lately, but I thought that was for a different reason.'

'What other reason?' he said blankly, adding salt to the wound. 'All I could think of lately were my plans for the new riverside complex.' His mouth twisted. 'In case you're interested, Athena turned them down.'

Joss stared at him in horrified sympathy. 'Peter—I'm so sorry! I know how hard you worked.' She frowned. 'But it isn't the end of the world, surely?'

'Of mine, with this particular firm of architects, it most definitely *is*.' Peter shrugged his shoulders moodily. 'Not that it matters. I was never cut out for corporate cut and thrust, Joss. I only took the job in the first place because you pushed me into it. I'm going back to the family firm. Where I belong,' he added as the crowning touch. He glanced at his watch, then caught her eye and flushed. 'I'm in no rush, Joss,' he said quickly. 'I can catch a later train.'

'Don't alter your arrangements on my account!' She stood with arms folded. 'I assume this means it's all over between us?'

Peter swallowed convulsively. 'I suppose it does.'

'You *suppose*?'

'I left you a letter, Joss,' he said hurriedly. 'It explains everything.'

'How thoughtful.' She eyed him with scorn. 'So if I'd come home at the usual time I would have found the bird flown?'

'I thought it would be easier that way,' he muttered, and handed her a cup of tea.

Joss slammed it down on a shelf. 'Easier for you, certainly, Peter.'

He shrugged sulkily. 'All right. Easier for me. Look, Joss, things haven't been right between us for a long time.' He squared his slim shoulders and looked her in the eye. 'If you want the truth, I'm just not happy with you anymore. You're older than me, more ambitious, you earn more money—hell, you're even taller than me. You—you diminish me, Joss. I can't take it any longer.'

'I see.' Joss's eyes burned angrily in her pale face. 'So that's it? The past year means nothing at all to you?'

'Is it only a year?' he said with unconscious cruelty. 'I thought it was longer than that. Anyway, I'm sorry it had to end like this. A pity you came home before I could—'

'Sneak away?' she said scathingly.

'Don't Joss! Let's part friends—please,' he pleaded, and put his hand on her arm.

She flung it away, suddenly unable to bear his touch. 'Just take your things and go, Peter. A pity my timing was wrong. You could have got away scot-free.'

He stepped back in quick offence. 'So why *were* you early?'

Joss clenched her teeth. 'I just felt like it. Goodbye, Peter.'

He moved towards her, arms outstretched, but backed away in a hurry as he met the look in her eyes. 'Goodbye, then, Joss. I—I wish things could have been different. If I'd won the Athena job—'

'I would still be older than you—and taller.' Her mouth twisted. 'I never dreamed it mattered so much.'

'In the beginning it didn't,' he muttered.

Joss locked militant eyes with his. 'Peter, tell me the truth. You owe me that much.'

He frowned. 'I *have* told the truth. Hell, I thought I'd even been a bit over the top with it. I never meant to come out with all that stuff about your age—and the height and so on.'

She shrugged impatiently. 'Never mind all that. Just tell me if there's someone else.'

'Another woman? Lord, no,' said Peter, with unmistakable candour. 'You've always been more woman than I can really handle, Joss. Never had any time—or energy—for anyone else.'

Joss looked across at Adam, taking comfort from the fierce look of distaste in his eyes. 'Oddly enough, that was the last straw. I lost it completely, made a terrible scene, threw my ring at him and sent him packing. Then I rang a removal firm and arranged to ship most of his belongings to his parents.' Her mouth twisted. 'Which is why I'm a bit lacking in home comforts. All the furniture was Peter's, but I've kept the sofa and the bed until—until I buy replacements.'

Adam gave her a probing look. 'You've kept all this secret?'

'Yes. No one knows yet, other than you.'

'Not even your parents?'

'I don't have any now. And I just couldn't spoil things for Anna before the party. I told her Peter was away on a course and couldn't come. She lives in Warwickshire, so it was easy to keep it from her for a while.'

'No wonder you weren't in party mood,' he said dryly.

She pulled a face. 'One way and another the party was a bit hard to take. Eventually the effort to sparkle was too much, so I spotted that deserted little balcony and vanished for a bit.'

Adam smiled a little. 'In the circumstances I'm surprised you were so polite when I joined you.'

Joss smiled back guiltily. 'My first reaction was to snarl and tell you to get lost. But after a while I was glad of your company. It kept me from wallowing in self-pity. It was gallant of you to come to my rescue.'

Adam shook his head. 'I'm no knight in shining armour, Eve. If the damsel in distress had been less pleasing to the eye I might have felt the same sympathy, but I doubt I'd have done anything about it.'

'An honest man!'

'I try to be. I watched your every move from the moment I first saw you. When you did your vanishing trick I seized the moment, grabbed two glasses of champagne and followed you outside.'

Her eyes danced. 'What would you have done if a vengeful husband had come after you?'

'Beaten a hasty retreat.' He grinned. 'I steer clear of husbands, vengeful or otherwise. I prefer my women unattached.'

'Your women?' Joss repeated.

'A figure of speech.'

Her eyes narrowed suddenly. 'Are *you* unattached, by the way?'

'Yes,' he said with emphasis. 'Otherwise this wouldn't be happening.'

'Would you like some coffee?' she said unevenly, very much aware that something *was* happening.

'Is that a polite way of asking me to go?'

Joss gave him a long, considering look. 'No,' she said quietly. 'Not if you'd like to stay awhile.'

'You know I would. And I don't want any more coffee,' he said deliberately. 'Shall I tell you what I do want?'

'No—please,' said Joss swiftly. 'Before Peter and I began to live together we'd been exclusive to each other for a fair time. I'm out of practice at this sort of thing.'

'What ''sort of thing'' do you think this is?' he asked, amused.

'More to the point, what do *you* think it is?'

'A simple desire to get to know you. How about you?'

Joss thought about it, fairly sure that 'simple' was the last word to describe her guest. 'I asked you here for a meal because I was depressed and angry, and you were kind and—'

'A lot taller than you,' he finished for her, and Joss laughed, suddenly more at ease.

'You're taller than most people!'

'I've never had more cause to be thankful for it than right now,' he assured her. 'So, mysterious Eve, come and sit beside me and hold my hand.'

'Ah, but if I give you my hand will you want more than that?'

'Yes,' he said bluntly. 'I'm male, and normal. But where women are concerned I don't take, Eve, only accept.'

'In that case...' Joss moved from her cushion to sit beside him on the sofa, discovering that the space left by his large frame was only just enough to accommodate her. 'A tight fit,' she said breathlessly.

Adam shifted slightly to give her more room, and took her hand in his. 'You were right,' he said after a moment.

'Just holding your hand isn't enough. Go back to your cushion.'

'Just how much else did you have in mind?' Joss asked very bluntly.

For answer Adam slid his arm round her. 'Only this.'

Joss laid her head against his shoulder, reassured, and the hard arm pulled her closer. It was new, and morale-boosting, to feel small and fragile in a man's embrace. She leaned against him, feeling safe and protected, his warmth soothing the anger and hurt of Peter's abrupt departure from her life.

'Why the sigh?' he asked.

'I was thinking how strange it was to be here like this with a man I'd never met until a few hours ago.'

'But you're no longer afraid of me,' he commented.

'I wasn't *afraid* of you,' she said indignantly, turning her face up to his.

He smiled down into her eyes. 'Nervous, then?'

'Yes.' She smiled back.

'Are you nervous now?'

'No.'

'So how *do* you feel?'

'Comfortable.'

His crack of laughter disarmed her completely. 'Not very flattering.'

'For me, tonight, it's the most flattering compliment I could pay you,' she said with feeling.

He raised the hand he was holding to his lips, and kissed it. 'If it's any consolation, I think the absconding fiancé's a complete idiot. But I'm grateful to him.'

'Why?'

'If he hadn't left I wouldn't be here.'

'True.' Joss yawned suddenly. 'Sorry,' she said with contrition. 'I haven't slept much lately.'

Adam smoothed her head down against his shoulder again. 'Relax,' he whispered in her ear, and Joss closed her eyes, melting against him pliantly.

She woke from a doze to find herself in Adam's arms *en route* to her bedroom. He bent slightly to open the door, then laid her on the bed and stood looking down at her.

'Goodnight, Eve,' he whispered, and bent to kiss her cheek.

Joss deliberately tilted her head so that the kiss landed squarely on her mouth, and suddenly the overwhelming need to feel whole and normal and desirable again obliterated caution. 'Don't go,' she said unsteadily. 'Don't leave me. Just for tonight. Please?'

Joss stared up in entreaty into the taut face, saw him close his eyes and clench his fists for an instant. Then he let out an unsteady breath, sat down on the bed and lifted her onto his lap, his forehead against hers.

'This wasn't meant to happen, Eve.'

'Don't you want me?' she said desolately.

'You know damn well I do!' he growled.

'Then show me.'

He locked his arms round her, pressing light, tantalising kisses at the corners of her mouth, but the contact ignited heat which rose in them both so quickly he was soon kissing her with a hunger which showed beyond all doubt how much he wanted her. She kissed him back, exulting in the desire she could feel vibrating through his body as he pulled her hard against him. Their kisses grew wilder, open-mouthed, tongues caressing as his hands sought breasts which rose taut with invitation in response. His breath rasped in his broad chest as he pulled away slightly to shrug off his jacket and tear his tie loose. Joss burrowed her face against him, her seeking hands undoing shirt buttons to find smooth skin hot to the touch. Darts of fire shot through her as she felt him hard and ready beneath her thighs, then he stood her on her feet and Joss backed away from him, her eyes locked with his in the semi-darkness. Slowly she slid the dress down her body, deliberate in her intention to inflame. She stepped out of the pooled silk and lace, then bent slowly to detach black silk suspenders from sheer dark stockings, and in triumph heard the hiss of his breath before he seized her, his mouth hard on hers as he dispensed with their remaining garments. At last he lifted her high in his arms, his eyes blazing with such need she shivered in excitement, and hid her hot face against his throat as he laid her on the bed.

'Are you sure?' he said harshly, in the moment before the question was too late. Joss nodded vehemently and stretched up her arms, pulling him down to her, and he stretched his long body beside her and slid his hands down her back to smooth her against him, their hearts thudding in perfect unison at the contact. Joss made a small, choked sound of protest as he put her away a little, then gasped in delight as he began to kiss every curve and hollow of her tall, slender body. The relentless, controlled caresses kindled slow fire along every nerve until Joss was in such an unashamed state of arousal that he abandoned the control, his hands and mouth so demanding they took her to dizzying heights of response. She surged against him, her fingers digging into the taut muscles of his broad shoulders, and he raised himself on his hands, his arms throbbing with the desire surging through his body. He asked a brief, urgent question and she shook her head wildly, and at last his body took possession of hers with a thrust of pure sensation, and she gasped, overwhelmed by fiery, rhythmic pleasure which mounted in increasing levels of intensity until white-hot culmination engulfed them both.

'What does one say in these circumstances?' she panted afterwards, when his arms had slackened slightly.

'What do you usually say?' Adam said hoarsely.

'Goodnight, I suppose.'

He raised his head to peer down into her face. 'Is that what you want *me* to say?'

'No.' Her eyes fell. 'Unless you want to go now.'

He kissed her hard. 'No, I don't want to go. I want to stay here, holding you in my arms all night, and maybe pinching myself from time to time to make sure this is real.'

'I feel like that,' she confessed. 'Shocked, too.'

'Shocked at what we did?'

'No,' she said dryly. 'I know about the birds and the bees.'

He laughed and kissed her again more gently, running the tip of his tongue over her lips. 'So what are you shocked about?'

'That I could have actually begged you to make love to me.' Joss bit her lip. 'I've never done that before.'

'I'm sure you haven't,' he said, his broad chest vibrating with laughter.

'I'm glad you find it so amusing!'

'Extraordinary, not amusing,' he assured her huskily. 'If you hadn't asked me to make love to you it's possible I might have found the strength to kiss you goodnight and leave, but I seriously doubt it. I wanted you from the moment I first saw your reflection in the mirror tonight.'

'Are you saying that to make me feel better?'

Adam smiled down into her eyes. 'No. It's the simple truth.'

Joss sighed with satisfaction, her mouth curving in a

smile he bent to kiss, taking his time over it. When she could speak she put a finger on his lips. 'You've achieved something rather wonderful tonight.'

'Don't I know it!'

'Not that,' she said impatiently, then smiled. 'Well, yes, that too, because it *was* wonderful. But the *way* you made love to me healed my poor, battered ego.'

'What way?' he asked, frowning.

'As though you were starving and I was food.' Joss blushed in the semi-darkness as he chuckled and ran his hands down the curve of her hips.

'That's it exactly,' he assured her. 'For me the entire evening was one long build-up of foreplay. Before I'd kissed this mouth, or caressed these exquisite breasts, all I could think of was this—and this—'

Adam matched caresses to his words with such skill desire swiftly engulfed them again, sending them in another breathtaking, headlong rush towards ecstasy.

CHAPTER THREE

AT SOME time in the night Joss was aware of hands pulling the covers over her, of a warm, hard mouth on hers for an instant, and a whispered goodnight in her ear, then she slept again until daylight brought her back to earth with a bump.

For a moment, as bright sunlight poured across the bed, she wondered if she'd dreamed the prolonged, sensual fantasy of the night.

But one look at the wild disorder of the bed told her it had all been blazingly real. A violent tremor ran through Joss at the thought of it. She breathed in deeply, pushed back the tangled covers and got out, raked tousled hair out of her eyes, restored a couple of pillows to their rightful place, then pulled on a dressing gown and ventured into the hall to make sure Adam had gone. When she found she was alone in the flat, Joss let out a deep, shaky breath. She hugged her arms across her chest, her face on fire at the memory of her utter abandon in the dark. She knew people who indulged in one-night stands without turning a hair. But it just wasn't her style. Last night had been a first on several counts. Living and sleeping with the man she'd expected to share her life with for ever had been no preparation for the bliss experienced in the arms of a total stranger.

There are names for women like you, Joss told herself darkly, and went off to run a hot bath. She lay in it for a long time, deep in thought, devoutly thankful that no one had actually seen her with Adam. If she were careful enough last night could remain a secret. She was unlikely to bump into her mystery lover again, whoever he was. Not that his identity mattered. Overpoweringly attractive he might be, but after her recent exit from the frying pan she had no intention of tumbling straight into the fire again, with Adam or anyone else. Joss got out of the bath, wincing as certain muscles protested in ways that brought colour to her face to think of them. She dressed hurriedly, and went into the kitchen, then stopped dead as she saw the note propped against the kettle.

Eve, it's damnably hard to tear myself away, but you might prefer to be alone when you wake. I'm out of the country for a few days. I'll ring when I get back. Adam.

Heat surged inside Joss. Shaken by the sheer, physical force of it, she fought hard against temptation. Last night, she told herself fiercely, had happened solely because Peter had left her devastated. Adam had restored her faith in herself quite miraculously. Their glorious night together had been a fitting climax to part of her life. But now it was time to get on with the rest of it. Besides, if she saw Adam again there would be no more mystery. Hard facts would be required about names and careers. So if he rang she would no longer be here. There had been a strong, sudden magic about last night. But magic couldn't be expected to last, or even happen twice. Joss hugged her arms across her chest to steady her thudding heart. Adam was a man of powerful charisma, and in her vulnerable state his passionate lovemaking had provided a quite wonderful salve for her bruised self-esteem. The Eve part of her longed to see him again. But realistic Joss knew that what seemed so irresistibly romantic in the hours of darkness might seem very different if they met again in the harsh light of day.

Early next morning Joss was packed and ready when the removal firm came to take her belongings away. One of the sub-editors on the *Post* had been searching for a flat in Notting Hill for months. After Peter's departure Joss had neither wanted nor could afford to live in the flat alone, and so had asked Nick Holt if he and Carrie fancied exchanging their flat in Acton for hers. The Holts had jumped at the chance, and the exchange was carried out at top speed. The new address was less fashionable, but the flat was in good repair, carried a much smaller price tag, and had no memories of Peter—or Adam—to haunt it.

The removal men had finished loading her belongings into the service lift and Joss was about to leave when a youth came hurrying towards her, holding a florist's box.

'Miss Eve?' he asked.

Joss opened her mouth to say no, then flushed and said yes.

'These are for you, then. They should have arrived earlier—bit of a problem with the greenery.'

Joss thanked him, and gave him a tip. The box held a sheaf of yellow roses on a bed of leaves. Fig leaves, she realised, her heart hammering. *'From Adam'*, said the card, and Joss buried her face in the blooms, suddenly engulfed in the memory of a hard, possessive body taut with desire, of skilled, caressing hands and gratifying, devouring kisses... She shivered, eyes tightly shut for a moment, then took in a deep, steadying breath, blotting out the memory by sheer strength of will. Then she closed the door and locked away a year of her life.

Her new home occupied the upper floor of an

Edwardian house in a picturesque terrace of identical houses in varying states of restoration and repair. It was much smaller than the flat in Notting Hill, but it would need less furniture, had a separate front door and private stairs, a forecourt to park the car, and, best of all, left Joss in possession of a sizeable sum of money. Part of this would go to Peter, to cover his half of the deposit on the expensive Notting Hill flat he'd insisted on, due to its superior architecture and fashionable address. But Joss had paid off the mortgage.

Once the removal men had gone Joss telephoned for a pizza, then rang Anna to give her the new phone number.

'I wish I could be there to help,' said Anna. 'Has Peter taken time off to give you a hand?'

'No,' said Joss, taking a deep breath. 'Look, Anna, are you busy? I've got something to tell you.'

Joss put the phone down later, feeling drained. Anna had blown her top, said a great many uncomplimentary things about Peter Sadler, congratulated Joss on being rid of such a poisonous rat, then offered to drive up to London that minute to provide a shoulder for her friend to cry on.

Joss had refused affectionately. 'I'll soon get used to being single again. I'll be fine. Don't worry, Anna.'

'I do worry,' said her friend stormily. 'Hugh was right. He never liked Peter. Anyway, did you enjoy the party?'

'Of course I did. By the way, who was that very tall man I saw with you when people were leaving?'

'Which one? I hadn't met half of Hugh's friends before.'

'I think this one was more a friend of a friend.'

'Shall I ask Hugh?'

'No, don't bother. Anyway, I must go. My lunch has arrived.'

Once she'd eaten her pizza, Joss locked up and went shopping for furniture. She ordered a comfortable sofa and pair of tables to hold her lamps, chose a restored brass bed, and arranged for delivery. Then she turned her attention to food. Her unexpected guest had demolished all the provisions bought to tide her over the move. Which was hardly surprising. There was a lot of him to keep fuelled. Joss thrust groceries in a basket at random, controlling a shiver at another memory of Adam's naked body. Making love with him, she told herself trenchantly, had happened purely because he'd materialised in her life at a time when she desperately needed to feel wanted and desirable again. And though Adam had fulfilled the need, with success so spectacular it overshadowed anything experienced with Peter, she had no intention of seeing him again.

When she got back to the flat Joss put the food away in the new fridge, then collected some tools together and began putting up her bookshelves, allowing herself to admit, at last, that her relationship with Peter had been foundering for some time. He had been all too accurate about their love-life, if she were brutally honest. It had been non-existent on a physical plane for a long time, and his failure to win the Athena contract had merely given him the excuse to break their engagement. But not the bottle to do it face to face. His dismay had been almost laughable when she'd turned up before he could sneak away.

At first Joss had been consumed with hurt and anger. Then fiercely grateful for the work which filled her life. She worked long, irregular hours as a freelance journalist, and regularly filled in for staff on holiday, or sick, or away on special assignments. Her free time had rarely coincided with Peter's, something he'd fiercely resented.

And there'd also been the burning question of a family. She had been adamant about waiting until he earned enough money for her to work less, and do more from home. And though he'd said he was agreeable Peter had obviously lied. As she should have realised. Everything Peter wanted he wanted right now.

Her eyes hardened. In the unlikely event that she ever considered a relationship with a man again she would make sure their aims were mutual. Her experience with Peter had taught her a salutary lesson. Any man in her future must fit certain requirements. He would be older, for a start, equally ambitious, and so successful in his own career he wouldn't resent hers. Joss smiled cynically. If such a paragon existed he was certain to be married anyway, to a stunningly beautiful woman who was a perfect wife and mother and ran her own thriving business while helping with the children's homework and producing cordon bleu dinners for twelve.

Joscelyn Hunter's interest in journalism had first begun when she'd edited the school magazine, which had fired her with such enthusiasm she'd found a job working at weekends and as holiday relief on the local morning paper. She'd started out as a messenger, then progressed to researcher, and soon begun bombarding the editor with so many stories and features he'd eventually accepted one, and she'd never looked back. She had been in her element mixing with journalists, so interested in all aspects of the job she'd made contacts which had won her a full-time job on the same paper, after she had a degree in modern languages and a year's post-graduate course in journalism under her belt.

At first Joss had loved her job, and with undiminished enthusiasm had covered law courts, local government, industry, the arts and a variety of local events. She'd interviewed a wide range of people, from local members of parliament, county councillors, businessmen, victims of tragedy, to schoolchildren and celebrities of all kinds. But after three years or so Joss had begun to feel inhibited by parochial bias. She'd lusted after a job on a national paper, and in her spare time had regularly submitted features to London dailies. When her efforts had begun to be accepted she'd taken the plunge and left for the capital, where her experience, coupled with the right qualifications and a willingness to work long, irregular hours, had won her jobs as a freelance, doing shiftwork on some of the national dailies.

Joss had set off for London with her father's blessing and a small legacy left by her mother. But soon afterwards the Reverend George Hunter had died, shortly before his retirement, leaving a grief-stricken Joss without a base in the Warwickshire village of her birth, other than her constant welcome from Anna's family. But her visits to the Herricks had been few and far between since her relationship with Peter, who had never fitted in with them. Now he was gone she could please herself, and would definitely drive down to Glebe House for lunch one day soon, Joss decided, preferably on one of the Sundays likely to drag a bit from now on.

Once she was settled in the new flat Joss steeled herself to forget Adam—and Peter—and soon found she quite enjoyed living alone. Her job absorbed most of her time, as usual, but now she could suit herself about what time she finished, with no reproaches when she got home, late and tired, to someone expecting her to cook supper and iron shirts. There were definite advantages to being single again.

As a change from reporting on press conferences, demonstrations, or whatever event the news editor wanted covered, one day Joss was told to dig out information about ancestral homes hired out by their owners for corporate entertaining, and spent time consulting with the *Daily Post* library and electronic database to discover which aristocratic personalities and properties were likely to be most newsworthy.

'We've got some mail for you,' said Carrie Holt, when Joss was poring over her findings with a lunchtime sandwich. 'And a message on the machine when we got home last night.' She handed over a bundle of junk mail and a slip of paper. 'How are you settling in at the flat?'

'Very well,' said Joss with satisfaction. 'How about you and Notting Hill?'

'I love it. I don't know how you could bear to leave the place, Joss.' Carrie bit her lip. 'Sorry. I'm a tactless cow. I suppose it was painful once Peter left.'

The message Carrie gave her was brief. *'I'm back. Ring me at this number. Adam.'*

Joss wanted to. Badly. But if she did ring him, Adam, like any man with blood in his veins, would expect to take up where he'd left off. Half of her wanted that so much it made her shake in her shoes, but the other half wouldn't hear of it. Peter's treatment had left her so vulnerable it would be madness to plunge into a new relationship. Her mood had been abnormally emotional with Adam that magical night. But she was back to normal now. And normal didn't include making mad, passionate love with strangers.

But when her phone rang late that night Joss felt oddly disappointed when she found it was just Anna, checking up on her.

'Are you pining, Joss?'

'No way. Too busy.'

'Is everything spick and span at the new place?'

'Hardly! I've only just got delivery of the new furniture, so the place is a mess. Who do you think I am, Superwoman?'

'Leave it all where it is and come down to stay with us instead.'

Joss was deeply tempted. 'I'd just love to, but the place is a shambles, Anna. I really must soldier on,' she said with regret. 'I'll come down as soon as I'm a bit straighter.'

'I'll keep on until you do,' threatened Anna, then went on to talk of wedding plans, and afterwards asked what Joss was up to at work, her interest caught when she heard about the article on ancestral homes.

'One of Hugh's old schoolfriends does that. He was at the party. Francis something. I'll tell Hugh to give him a call.'

Next day Joss spent a morning on the phone, setting up interviews with the owners of various ancestral piles she'd decided on for her article, then settled down to one of the more mundane tasks of the freelance journalist, and began sifting through a pile of regional newspapers looking for stories that could be followed up on a national basis. When her phone rang Joss was heartily glad to be interrupted.

'Miss Hunter?' asked a light, attractive male voice. 'My name's Francis Legh. Hugh Wakefield rang last night, asked me to get in touch. What can I do for you?'

Hugh's old schoolfriend, Joss learned, was only too pleased to be part of her story on corporate entertaining.

'Publicity of the right kind never goes amiss,' he assured her.

'Would it be possible for me to see you this week?' asked Joss hopefully. 'Where exactly do you live?'

'Deep in the wilds of Dorset. Do you know the area?'

'Not very well, but if you give me the address I'll find you.'

'I don't suppose you could possibly come on Sunday, Miss Hunter?' he asked. 'We're having some fancy electronics installed during the week. On the other hand,' he added suddenly, 'it's colossal cheek to ask you to give up your time on a weekend—'

'Not at all. I'd be glad to,' said Joss quickly. 'What time shall I come?'

'Midday,' he said promptly. 'I'll give you lunch.'

The news editor buttonholed her shortly afterwards, with the news that Charlotte Tracy, who covered all the smart events of the season, had rung in to say she was going home early from Ascot with flu.

'Flu in June,' said Jack Ormond bitterly. 'How the hell did she manage that? Anyway, Joss, it means you'll have to cover Ladies' Day at the races tomorrow. Thank goodness you can handle a camera—you know the happy-snappy kind of thing Charlotte turns in.'

'You bet,' she said with enthusiasm. But no way was she going to Ascot in her normal working gear of trouser suit and T-shirt. She was due at Harrods later, to interview a movie star at a book signing. Afterwards she would dash along the road to Harvey Nichols, splurge on an outfit for Anna's wedding and wear it to Ascot first.

After her chat with the actress Joss rang in her brief report to accompany the glamour shot waiting to go with it, then spent an hour on choosing a bronze silk suit and large, flattering hat in creamy translucent straw. It's for Anna, she reminded herself, wincing as she signed the credit card slip.

For once the British summer turned up trumps and favoured Ladies' Day with glorious sunshine. Joss found

a good place in the crowd at the rail in front of Tattersalls
to watch the procession of carriages bearing the Queen
and various members of the royal family, and afterwards
wandered among the elegant crowds, murmuring dis-
creetly into her little machine, pausing now and then to
photograph a particularly adventurous creation. It was the
outlandish which made news, and Joss snapped away at
towering feathered confections and precarious architec-
tural fantasies, glad for once of her height as she jostled
to get a clear shot.

Towards the end of the afternoon Joss had seen quite
enough hats to last her for life, and decided to take one
last shot of the horses in the starting gate instead, then
leave to beat the rush. Before she could get her shot in
focus someone jostled her elbow, and instead of a row
of snorting horseflesh she found she was looking through
the viewfinder at the top half of a man who towered
above the crowd. Joss stood rooted to the spot, her heart
thumping at the discovery that Adam looked even better
by daylight in morning coat and top hat, an opinion obviously shared by the woman gazing up at him raptly
from under the brim of a sensational feathered creation.
On impulse Joss snapped the striking pair, then pushed
her way through the crowd before she was spotted, all
her pleasure in the day gone. Seen in daylight, in all the
glory of formal Ascot wear, Adam was even more impressive than she remembered. No wonder she'd wanted
him to make love to her. But so did his beautiful companion by the look on her face. The pair of them had
been obviously engrossed in each other. Joss drove back
to London in a black mood, and snarled irritably at the
wolf-whistles and lip-smacking which greeted her finery
when she plunged back into the usual frenzy at the *Post*.

For most of the next day Joss found it hard to put

Adam and his lady from her mind. How smug she had
been, she fumed bitterly, about her virtue in avoiding
another meeting. So smug she had no right to such irra-
tional, mortifying jealousy. But because of it Friday
seemed interminable, and when it was over at last Joss
did her best to put Adam from her mind by spending a
couple of lively, unwinding hours over a meal in a wine
bar with a bunch of fellow journalists before she finally
went home.

'Joss,' said Carrie Holt's indignant voice on the an-
swer-machine. '*Two* messages tonight. One from Peter
and another from this mysterious Adam person. For
pity's sake give the men in your life your new number.'

Joss bit her lip. The Holts had every right to be annoyed. She would drop a line to Peter and tell him she'd
moved, and not to get in touch again. Adam she would
ring right now. She tapped in the number, then sat, tense,
on the edge of the bed while she waited for him to answer. But the only response was a terse recorded message
stating his number and a request for the caller's identity.
For a moment Joss was so shattered by disappointment
she couldn't speak. Then she pulled herself together and
said coldly,

'This is Eve. I've moved from the flat in Notting Hill.
To make an entirely new start. In every way,' she added
with emphasis. 'Thank you for the beautiful roses, and
for your—your kindness that night. Goodbye.'

When Joss reached Dorchester on Sunday, she skirted
it, as directed, and after a few miles turned off on a minor
road which took her straight into the rolling, deeply cleft
terrain familiar to fans of Thomas Hardy novels. With
time to spare she drove slowly, to appreciate her surroundings, but eventually spotted a sign for Eastlegh
Hall, home of Francis Legh, who, she'd discovered from

research beforehand, was the ninth Baron Morville to live there. Joss turned in through a pair of beautiful gates and drove along a carriageway that wound through tree-dotted parkland for a considerable distance before approaching a rise crowned by Eastlegh Hall, which gleamed in pale, Palladian splendour in the sun.

Hugh's friend would have very little trouble letting this beauty out for conferences, or anything else, thought Joss, impressed. She walked up a flight of shallow stone steps to the terrace, and crossed to the pillared portico, where large doors stood open, giving a view of a lofty hall with a pair of carved chests and a pedestal holding an urn overflowing with fresh flowers. She lifted the ornate knocker on one of the doors, then waited on the threshold, admiring the burnished dark wood of the graceful double staircase, and eventually a slim, well-dressed woman emerged from a door at the back of the hall and came hurrying towards her.

'Miss Hunter? Lord Morville apologises for being held up. He suggests I show you over the house while you're waiting. I'm Elizabeth Wilcox, the housekeeper.'

'How do you do?' Joss smiled warmly. 'Thank you. I'd like that very much.'

'We'll just take a quick tour,' said Mrs Wilcox. 'Lord Morville will show you the rest after lunch.'

Joss followed her guide through a series of beautiful rooms hung with paintings, a formal drawing room with pale yellow walls and gilt and damask furniture, a double-cube salon, a ballroom with a painted ceiling, and a dining room with sweeping velvet curtains, swagged and tasselled in gold, and a table long enough to seat thirty at a push. The grand staircase led to a long gallery hung with more paintings, and formal bedrooms with four-posters.

'Few stately homes are able to offer overnight facilities of the type available at Eastlegh. We even have central heating in some parts,' added Mrs Wilcox proudly. 'Installed by Lord Morville's American grandmother.'

'It's all very impressive, and so well kept,' said Joss with respect.

'Thank you. I'm lucky to have a good team.' The housekeeper smiled, gratified, then looked at her watch. 'Now I'll show you how to get to the farm.'

'Farm?' said Joss, surprised.

The other woman smiled regretfully. 'Lord Morville no longer lives in the house. He moved into Home Farm when his father died.'

Following the housekeeper's directions, Joss drove past a formal knot garden and skirted a maze, then drove along a carriageway through woodland until a large house with barleystick chimneys came into view above box hedges which enclosed its gardens in privacy. Joss parked the car, then opened a tall wrought-iron gate and followed a paved path through beds filled with roses. Before she could knock on the massive oak door it was flung open by a fair, smiling man in jeans and checked shirt.

'Lord Morville?' Joss smiled. 'I'm Joscelyn Hunter.'

'Francis, please,' he said quickly, holding out his hand, grey eyes friendly in a long, attractive face easily recognisable from some of the portraits in the Hall. 'Sorry I wasn't on hand when you arrived, Miss Hunter. We were sorting out a problem with the latest booking.'

Wondering if the 'we' meant Lady Morville was on hand, she smiled, liking him on sight. 'I'm usually Joss.'

'Then Joss it shall be.' He led the way through a square, stone-flagged hall into a sitting room with panelled walls, comfortable chintz-covered furniture and a massive stone fireplace. He waved her to a chair, then crossed to a tray of drinks. 'What can I give you?'

'Something long, cold and non-alcoholic, please,' said Joss, smiling, pleased that the long journey had dictated her choice of clothes. Her fawn linen trousers and plain white shirt were in perfect keeping with her casually dressed host.

'I thought we'd have lunch first,' he said, handing her a tall ice-filled glass. 'Then we can go back to the house and you can ask what questions you like. Or you can ask some now.'

'I was surprised to find you don't actually live at Eastlegh,' said Joss. 'Did you find it strange, moving to a much smaller house?'

'Not in the least.' He grinned. 'When I was young I was never allowed in the state rooms anyway, and the bedrooms here are a damn sight more comfortable than my old room over at the house.'

He looked up as a young woman came into the room. 'Ah, Sarah, this is Miss Hunter from the *Daily Post*.'

Sarah was composed and dark-haired, and oddly familiar, with a swift, charming smile. 'Hello. I'm Sarah Wilcox.'

Not Lady Morville, then. Joss smiled and took the proffered hand. 'Hello. I assume I've just met your mother.'

'Yes. She loves showing Eastlegh off to visitors.'

'Between them the Wilcox family run my life,' said Francis. 'Elizabeth is housekeeper, as you already know. Her husband Alan acts as butler when necessary, and helps me run the estate, and their frighteningly well-qualified daughter here is my House Manager and executive right hand.' He turned to Sarah with a coaxing smile. 'Change your mind. Have lunch with us.'

'I'd love to,' she said regretfully, 'but I promised to share the family roast for once. I've heated Mrs Wyatt's soup for you. The vegetable flan is in the warming oven, and the rest is just salad, cold beef and cheese.'

'What would I do without you, Sarah?' he said warmly.

She smiled at him serenely, and turned to Joss. 'Francis will give you my extension number, so if you need any further information just ring me and I'll provide it.'

'A lot better than I can,' said Francis wryly.

Joss thanked her, then watched thoughtfully as Francis escorted his attractive right hand from the room. Sarah Wilcox might not be Lady Morville, but it was plain to the onlooker, if not to His Lordship, that she would like to be.

When Francis got back he topped up Joss's glass and told her Mrs Wyatt was the lady who looked after him during the week. 'I fend for myself on weekends, but when Sarah heard you were coming for lunch she insisted on organising it. Very efficient lady, young Sarah.'

'A very attractive one, too,' said Joss.

Francis looked blank. 'Sarah? Yes,' he said, surprised. 'I suppose she is.'

'Is this actually a working farm?' asked Joss.

'Not any more. I won't bore you with politics, but we gave up farming a few years ago as no longer feasible. But we do a roaring trade in shrubs and bedding plants, and every type of herb imaginable—and people come from miles around to buy Sam's organic vegetables.'

'Who's Sam?'

'Used to be head gardener at one time, officially now retired. But he still terrorises the groundstaff here. When I was a schoolboy I don't know who frightened me more,

Sam or my father. Ah, good.' Francis opened one of the windows and leaned out. 'Hurry it up, Dan, I'm hungry.' He turned back to Joss with a smile. 'I persuaded a friend of mine to join us for lunch. Let's go straight to the table.'

The dining room was across the hall, with more panelling, and a table set for three with a posy of flowers for centrepiece.

'Courtesy of Sarah?' asked Joss, then her smile congealed on her face as a man loomed in the doorway, ducking his head to enter the room. Instead of a formal suit he wore jeans and a thin dark blue shirt, but there was no mistaking his identity. Or the face which hardened to a mask at the sight of her.

'Perfect timing, Dan,' said Francis, grinning. 'Let me introduce Miss Joscelyn Hunter—Joss to her friends, she tells me. Joss, this is Daniel Armstrong.' He looked from one rigid face to the other, his eyes gleaming with curiosity. 'Ah! You two know each other already.'

CHAPTER FOUR

'WE'VE met,' agreed Dan Armstrong tightly. 'How are you—Miss Hunter?'

'Very well.' She smiled brightly, wondering if he could hear her heart banging against her ribs.

His eyes held hers relentlessly. 'Francis told me a journalist was coming to do an article on Eastlegh. Quite a surprise to discover it's you. What paper do you work for?'

'I freelance, but in this instance I'm working for the *Daily Post*.'

'The article Joss is doing will provide some welcome publicity,' said Francis, and waved Dan to a chair. 'Stop towering over us and sit down.' He fetched a tureen of soup from a hotplate and set it in front of Joss. 'Will you do the honours?'

Joss sent up a silent prayer of entreaty, and managed to fill three bowls without spilling a single drop of steaming vegetable soup, something she was rather proud of with a slanted, hostile gaze fixed on her throughout the operation.

'I gather you've moved to a new flat,' Dan observed as she passed him his bowl.

So he'd received her message. 'Yes.' She smiled at Francis. 'I'd been living in a flat in Notting Hill, but I moved recently. My new address is less smart, but a lot cheaper.'

'You forgot to mention the move last time we met,' said Dan without inflection.

'Did I?' said Joss casually. 'Some friends at the *Post* bought it.'

'Have you known each other long?' said Francis with interest. 'Dan's never mentioned you.'

'No, not long,' said Joss, her eyes on her soup.

'Unlike Dan and me,' said her host. 'We've known each other all our lives.'

'Really?' Joss looked up in polite enquiry. 'Do you still live in this part of the world, Mr Armstrong?'

'Not any more.' His eyes met hers head-on. 'But I was born in a cottage on the Eastlegh estate. My father was head gardener here until recently.'

'He still is in all but name,' said Francis, grinning. 'Dan's father is Sam Armstrong, the despot I was talking about earlier.'

Dan stiffened visibly. 'I'm surprised my family is of such interest.'

'Joss is interested in all aspects of Eastlegh for her article,' said Francis, looking down his nose. 'Your father's name came up due to his famous vegetables, Dan. He's as much part of Eastlegh as I am. You have a problem with that?'

Dan threw up a hand like a fencer, giving his friend a wry smile. 'No, milord, so get off your high horse.' He looked at Joss. 'But if you plan to mention my father in your article, Miss Hunter, I strongly advise asking his permission first.'

'I second that,' said Francis with feeling. 'All right for you two; you won't be here when he reads it. I will.'

'If he makes a fuss just look down your nose like that and remind him you're Lord Morville,' advised Dan dryly.

'Fat lot of use that would be! You know damn well

that as far as Sam's concerned my father was Lord Morville, and that's that.'

'Don't worry, I never write anything without the subject's permission,' said Joss hastily. 'If Mr Armstrong objects I won't mention him.'

'No!' said both men, with such force Joss stared in surprise.

'If you leave my father out of anything written about Eastlegh he'll make Francis's life a misery,' said Dan, smiling at her for the first time.

'Then of course I won't,' Joss assured them.

To her surprise both men got up, with the ease of long habit: Dan to take the plates, and Francis to serve the main course.

He grinned at her blank look. 'Did you expect a footman behind every chair?'

She smiled wryly. 'No, but I didn't expect you to wait on me in person.'

'Not much choice these days.' Francis shrugged. 'My problem is common among my breed. Asset-rich and cash-poor.'

'May I quote you on that?' she asked.

'Of course,' said Francis cheerfully, slicing a vegetable tart. He served Joss deftly, and offered a platter of rare roast beef. 'Can I tempt you?'

Joss refused, her appetite diminished by the presence of the man she must now think of as Daniel Armstrong. And think of him she would. She'd been a panicking fool to believe the magic of that night would vanish by daylight. Meeting him again only confirmed her reaction at Ascot. If he wanted to take up where he left off she would have no objection at all. But it was depressingly obvious that he had no such intention.

'You're very quiet, Miss Hunter,' he commented, startling her. 'For a journalist,' he added.

'Now then, Dan,' warned Francis. 'Don't get on your hobby horse.'

'He means I shun the attentions of the press,' said Dan, looking her in the eye.

'Dan tends to be a bit of a recluse,' explained Francis. 'Which is an odd trait for someone of his particular calling.'

'What exactly do you do, Mr Armstrong?' asked Joss, remembering his mention of construction work. And the picture it had conjured up.

'He's a property developer,' said Francis, grinning. 'He knocks down beautiful old buildings and puts up modern monstrosities in their place.'

'I don't knock them all down,' said Dan, unmoved.

'True. You work miracles on some of them,' conceded Francis. 'Dan and I went into banking together originally,' he informed Joss. 'We were good at it, made a bit of money with some fancy investments in the eighties. Then my father died, I had to come back to Eastlegh, and Dan started up his property company.'

'This is strictly off the record, Miss Hunter,' said Dan quickly, his eyes spearing hers. 'If I read an article on the theme of "gardener's son makes success in property world," I'll sue.'

'My mission concerns Lord Morville and Eastlegh,' said Joss loftily. 'Not,' she added, 'that you *could* sue, if it's the truth.'

'Got you there, old son,' chortled Francis, and rose to his feet. 'You stay and entertain Joss, Dan. I'll make coffee.'

When they were alone Dan got up and began transferring dishes from table to sideboard.

'Do you need any help?' asked Joss politely.

'No.' He sat down again, eyeing her with undisguised animosity. 'So, Joscelyn Hunter. This is an unexpected pleasure. For me, at least. Obviously not for you.'

'Why not?'

'You know damn well. Your message came over loud and clear!' He leaned forward, no longer troubling to hide his hostility now there was no one to see. 'It does damn all for a man's ego to be used like a bloody gigolo,' he said in a harsh undertone. 'And found wanting at that. When did you move?'

'The following day,' she said, fighting the urge to cower in her seat.

'So why keep me in the dark?' he demanded.

'Isn't it obvious? After—afterwards I was hideously embarrassed.' Her eyes fell before the hard glitter in his. 'It's not a habit of mine to behave like that.'

'Credit me with enough intelligence to know that. Look at me!' he ordered.

Joss raised her eyes reluctantly.

'The maidenly panic is unnecessary,' he said abrasively. 'It was *you* who asked me to make love to you, remember.'

'Which is the whole point!' she said with sudden passion. 'In the cold light of day I couldn't believe I'd done that. I just couldn't cope with meeting you face to face again.'

'Afraid I'd haul you off to bed the minute you opened the door?'

Her mouth compressed. 'Of course not,' she muttered.

He sat back, looking irritatingly relaxed. 'Or maybe I didn't come up to scratch as replacement for the absconding lover.' He shrugged negligently. 'Not that it matters. I don't aspire to the role.'

His words acted like a stomach punch. 'Then there's no harm done,' Joss snapped.

'By the way, I saw you at Ascot, fleetingly,' he said, startling her. 'As soon as I could I came after you, but you took off faster than the winner of the three-thirty. And vanished again. Did you see me?'

'No,' she lied huskily. 'I was working—' She looked up in relief, deeply grateful for the interruption when Francis backed into the room with a tray.

'Sorry I took so long,' he apologised. 'Hope you two managed to entertain each other?'

'Of course,' said Dan blandly. 'It's a long time since I enjoyed such an entertaining lunch. Thanks, Francis. Excellent meal, as always.'

'When I go up to his place he gets food sent in,' said Francis, pushing the tray towards Joss. 'We make sure he gets some home cooking when he honours us with a visit.'

Joss poured coffee with a gratifyingly steady hand, then smiled at Francis, pointedly ignoring his friend. 'When we've finished this could we make a start?'

Dan pushed his untouched cup aside and jumped to his feet, his eyes cold. 'I must go. It's been very interesting to meet you again, Miss Hunter. Goodbye.'

'Goodbye,' she said politely.

Francis excused himself to see his friend out, then rejoined Joss, looking perplexed. 'You two obviously don't get on very well.'

Remembering how spectacularly well they'd got on in one instance, Joss forced a smile. 'Maybe he didn't take kindly to breaking bread with a journalist.'

'Possibly,' conceded Francis, unconvinced.

Alone in a cloakroom at the back of the hall, Joss ran cold water on her wrists until she'd cooled down. Meeting the man she now knew to be Dan Armstrong had given her such a shock she'd failed to adjust to it right through lunch. Neither man had commented, but the food left on her plate must have given Dan *some* satisfaction, if he recalled the other meal they'd shared. She ground her teeth in frustration, then repaired her face, brushed her hair into place, and went to rejoin Francis.

Once they were in Eastlegh Hall together Joss soon discovered a shrewd, businesslike streak beneath the easy charm of its owner. Francis Legh, ninth Baron Morville, obviously loved his home with a passion. He was deliberately offhand when describing the fashionable Palladian façade one of his ancestors had thrown up around the original Tudor building, but unashamedly impassioned about his determination to hang on to his home, even if it meant moving out of it to do so.

'It costs so much to open it to the public it's better business to offer the entire house to corporations, banks or television companies who want it exclusive to themselves for whatever period their funds run to,' he informed her. 'Here, due to my darling Yankee grandma, we have relatively modern plumbing and heating, and some comfortably furnished bedrooms as well as the formal stateroom variety. The package I offer includes a room, dinner, plus early-morning tea and breakfast, supervised by Alan Wilcox in butler mode to impress.'

'With far more privacy than possible at a hotel,' said Joss, nodding.

'Exactly.' Francis led the way through a door opening off the ballroom. 'This used to be a music room. It's still a bit untidy, due to the alterations I mentioned. I've put in a new sound system, and at the touch of a button a screen descends from the ceiling.'

'I'm impressed,' Joss assured him. 'If I send a photographer down during the week, would you allow some pictures?'

'Of course—but only if I can vet them first,' he added quickly, and grinned. 'I sound like Dan.' He shot a searching look in her direction. 'Talking of Dan, why don't you like him?'

Joss shrugged. 'It's he who objects to me.'

'Because you're a journalist?'

'Your friend can tell you that better than I can,' she said tartly, then smiled at him in apology. 'Sorry. Didn't mean to be rude, Lord Morville.'

'My name's Francis,' he said gently. 'If you've seen all you want here perhaps you'd like a stroll outside. It's a beautiful afternoon.'

'Thank you, I'd like that very much.'

The present Lord Morville of Eastlegh so obviously loved every stick and stone and blade of grass of his property that Joss warmed to him more and more as they strolled through the afternoon sunshine. Eventually they left the gardens behind and made for the hothouses, where plants and shrubs were sold to the public.

'That's the house where Dan was born,' said Francis, pointing. 'Used to be a tied cottage, but Sam Armstrong owns it now.'

'You sold it to him?' said Joss, surprised. 'I thought people like you—' She halted, embarrassed.

'You thought that people like me hang onto every possible bit of land and property they possess,' he finished for her. 'They do. So do I, tooth and nail. But in this one instance I yielded to powerful persuasion.' He waved a hand towards the people milling round the hothouses. 'Sunday's a busy day at the nursery. The groundstaff sell Sam's produce there for him. Would you like to meet him?'

'Very much,' said Joss promptly.

But when they reached the cottage she hesitated.

'On the other hand I don't want to intrude. Your friend might disapprove if I barge into his father's house un-invited.'

'He won't disapprove of *me*,' said Francis, with the assurance of his pedigree. 'Besides, I mentioned it to Dan when he was leaving.'

The Armstrong home was very different from Joss's expectations. Tied cottage by name, in actual fact it was a house, and a surprisingly sizeable one. Her precon-ceived idea of thatch and roses round the door was a long way from the reality of a house built on a smaller scale than Home Farm, but otherwise identical in age and ar-chitecture.

The man who answered Francis's knock was older than Joss had expected, but instantly recognisable. The height and hawk-like features were the same. But the hair was white, and the lined face below it weathered to a hue much darker than his son's. Sam Armstrong wore a for-mal white shirt and tie with comfortable old corduroys and a fawn cardigan, and nodded, unsurprised, at the sight of them.

'Good afternoon to you both. Dan said you were com-ing over.'

'Hello, Sam,' said Francis cheerfully. 'Hope we're not disturbing you. This is Miss Joscelyn Hunter, a journalist from the *Daily Post*. She's come to do a piece on Eastlegh, so I said she couldn't possibly leave without talking to you.'

'How do you do, Mr Armstrong?' said Joss, holding out her hand.

It was clasped for an instant of contact with a rough, workworn palm. The shrewd blue eyes looked her over, then Sam Armstrong nodded, and stood aside to usher them into a cool, dark hall. 'Come in and have some tea.'

A small table under the window in the sitting room was laid with fine china and a dish of buttered scones. Dan stood erect by the fireplace, his body language stating very clearly that he was there on sufferance.

'You go and make the tea, Dan,' ordered his father. 'The kettle's on the boil.'

Stiff-backed, Dan excused himself and went out to do his parent's bidding, very much aware, by his rigid expression, that Joss was entertained by his role of dutiful son.

'Sit down, Miss Hunter,' said Sam.

Francis held out a dining chair for Joss, then perched himself on the stone window ledge and gave Joss time to examine her surroundings by engaging Sam in a conversation centred on asparagus. Two vast leather chairs flanked the fireplace in a room furnished with good, solid wood pieces very much in keeping with the home of a family which had served the masters of Eastlegh Hall for generations. Until Dan had broken the pattern.

'So you're going to do a piece about Eastlegh, Miss Hunter?' said Sam Armstrong.

Dan appeared with a teapot and set it down on the tray in front of Joss. 'My father doesn't approve of letting the Hall out to strangers, Miss Hunter.'

'Lord Morville wouldn't have liked it,' said the old man bluntly.

His son shot him a warning look. 'Lord Morville, Father, is taking tea with us at this moment.'

Sam Armstrong looked discomfited for a moment. 'I meant no offence,' he said gruffly.

'None taken, Sam,' Francis assured him, and helped

himself to a scone. 'Besides, you know that death duties gave me no choice.'

'I know, I know,' said Sam grudgingly. 'Will you pour the tea, miss?'

Joss complied, finding it no easier to fill cups than soup bowls with Dan looking on. He handed tea to Francis and his father, then took his own to the fireplace and stood there, listening in silence as Joss began to ask questions she soon found were superfluous. Sam was only too glad of an audience for his anecdotes.

He settled back in his chair, letting his tea cool. 'My forebears were reivers in the Borders—moss troopers, as they were called—'

'Cattle rustlers, actually,' interrupted Dan, and won himself a glare from his parent.

'My grandfather, Adam Armstrong,' resumed Sam, unaware of the name's impact on Joss, 'came down here looking for work. He was given a job in the stables, and eventually became head coachman.'

Adam Armstrong's son, Daniel, had preferred work with plants and soil to horses, and had worked his way up to the job of head gardener, a post taken over in time by Sam, his own son.

'Armstrongs have lived in this house for three generations,' Sam went on bitterly, 'but not any more. *My* son prefers London.'

'And I live in Home Farm instead of at the Hall,' put in Francis, aware that Dan was silently seething. 'Times change, Sam. We change with them or we go under.'

Sam turned to Joss. 'I watched these two run wild, miss. Master Francis—Lord Morville—lost his mother when he was a little lad, so he used to come here to my wife for cakes and spoiling—and bandaging up, often as not. They were always up to mischief, these two.'

'I don't think Miss Hunter needs to hear all this, Father,' said Dan stiffly.

'Why not? She must be wondering why the gardener's son is so pally with Lord Morville of Eastlegh,' said Sam, unmoved. He smiled at Joss. 'They went to different schools and different colleges, but it never made much difference.'

'Lacking any brothers of our own, we made do with each other,' said Francis matter-of-factly.

'Which is why I can't understand why the pair of you don't get married and start families of your own,' said Sam irritably.

'You may be retired, Father, but Francis is still Lord Morville. You just can't say things like that to him. And you forget you're in the presence of a journalist,' Dan reminded him. 'The absence of wives might start her wondering about our sexual preferences—'

'Speak for yourself, Dan!' said Francis heatedly.

'And remember there's a lady in the room,' thundered Sam.

Dan shrugged. 'Miss Hunter's a journalist,' he said flatly, making the implication very plain.

Joss swallowed the insult, and looked at Dan levelly. 'Don't worry, Mr Armstrong. I don't write a gossip column. My article centres on the ancestral homes I'm featuring and the commercial facilities offered by their owners. Other than your father, I'm more likely to bring in people like Sarah Wilcox than property developers with no relevance to the subject.'

'Actually, that's not true—' began Francis, then halted at the ferocious scowl Dan turned on him.

Joss got up, bringing Sam and Francis to their feet. 'Thanks for the tea, Mr Armstrong, and for sparing time to talk to me. It's been fascinating. I'll let Lord Morville know when the article's due to appear.' She shook Sam's hand, then turned to Dan. 'Goodbye, again.'

'Goodbye,' he said, looking down at her. He held out his hand. 'Perhaps we'll meet again.'

Joss put her hand in his for the barest instant, aware that Francis was looking on with undisguised interest. 'Perhaps,' she agreed.

Sam Armstrong went with Joss to the door, but Dan called Francis back for a moment, talking to him in urgent undertone. Wildly curious to know what Dan was saying to his friend, Joss duly admired the garden instead of trying to listen, thanked Sam Armstrong again, then walked back to Eastlegh Hall with Francis.

'Do you have enough for your article?' he asked as they reached her car.

Joss nodded. 'I certainly do. You've got a good thing going here. Thank you for letting me see it, and for giving me lunch.'

Francis fished out his wallet and took out a card. 'If you need more information contact me here at the Hall or at Home Farm. Sarah will find me if I'm missing.'

'Thank you. I'll let you know about the photographer.' Joss put the card in her handbag and held out her hand. 'Goodbye.'

He took it in his. 'And just in case I need it could I have your home number and address?'

Joss hunted in her bag and handed him a card, then got in the car and, with a final smile and wave, drove back through the parkland of Eastlegh Hall and made for the road to Dorchester. She made no effort to hurry, preferring to enjoy the beautiful summer evening at leisure rather than hurtle back to London. At one stage she stopped off for coffee at an inn roofed in the thatch typical of the area, and sat outside to drink it while she recovered from the shock of meeting Daniel Armstrong. A pity she'd left such a cold message on his phone. Not that it mattered. He'd obviously washed his hands of her when he'd found she'd moved. Nor, thought Joss, trying to be fair, could she blame him. He obviously felt he'd been tried and found wanting. Which was so far from the truth it was ludicrous. But she could never tell him that now.

As Joss neared London later the traffic was heavy, and after the strain of the day she was tired by the time she parked her car on the forecourt outside the house. She switched off the ignition, then gave a screech of fright as her door was yanked open.

'Where the devil have you been?' said Dan Armstrong irritably. 'You took your time.'

CHAPTER FIVE

HER heart hammering at the sight of him, Joss got out of
the car, slammed the door shut, locked it, then turned
hostile eyes up to his face. 'You told Lord Morville to
ask for my address,' she accused.

He shrugged. 'It was unlikely you'd give it to *me*.'

Joss glared at him, secretly cursing him for catching
her with a shiny face and windblown hair. 'So why are
you here?'

'I was just passing.' The slanted navy blue eyes
gleamed with a smile which set her teeth on edge.

'Very amusing,' snapped Joss, and put her key in the
door, then turned to face him. 'I'm tired, so I'll say goodnight.'

'Not so fast—I want to talk to you,' he said imperi-
ously. 'It won't take long. Ask me in. Or we can have
the conversation out here in the street. Your choice.'

Since Daniel Armstrong so very obviously meant what
he said, Joss gave in. 'Oh, very well.' She unlocked the
door and led the way up the stairs that led directly into
her new sitting room.

'I like this better than the other place,' said Dan, looking round him in approval. 'Sound investment.'

'Ah,' said Joss tartly. 'There speaks the property developer.'

Dan stood at the window, looking down at the street.
'You make those sound like dirty words.' He turned to
look at her. 'Francis was joking. If I do knock buildings
down they're derelict eyesores. And the others I put up

61

in their place are always sympathetic to their environment.'

'How interesting,' said Joss politely, hoping he couldn't tell how deeply she was affected simply by being alone with him again. And by the way his sheer presence dominated the room. She gestured at the boxes of books waiting for transfer to the shelves she'd put up. 'I'm afraid I'm not very tidy yet. And I've bought only the basic requirements, like this sofa and—and so on, but at least it's all my own. Won't you sit down?'

But Dan wasn't looking at the room. 'You look just as good in trousers as the sexy black dress,' he said, startling her.

'Thank you,' she said, swallowing. 'Can I give you a drink, or some coffee?'

'Aren't you curious to know why I came chasing after you?' he asked, moving closer.

Joss backed away. 'To vent your anger about my disappearing act?' she said curtly, annoyed because she felt flustered.

'I did that in Home Farm while Francis was making coffee.' He smiled slowly. 'Have you any idea how I felt when I found you sitting at his dining table?'

She nodded. 'Similar to my own reaction, I imagine—'

'I doubt it.' Dan moved nearer, and this time Joss stood her ground. 'I couldn't believe my eyes. For the first time in our long association I could have blacked Lord Morville's eye.'

'Why?' she demanded, half knowing the answer, yet afraid to believe it.

'Because it was a shock to find my elusive Eve in the last place I expected,' he said, his voice deepening. 'I was jealous. An emotion unknown to me before today.'

Joss cleared her throat, feeling breathless. 'I'd never

have known. You were so damn hostile you put me off my lunch.'

'I noticed!' His smile was so smug she wanted to hit him. 'It gave me great satisfaction to watch you pushing food round your plate.'

'Why?'

Dan took her hand and led her to the new sofa, which was larger and much better suited to his proportions than the old one. 'Sit down while I explain.'

Wishing her funds had run to a matching chair, Joss sat, leaving as much space as possible for her unexpected guest. 'Explain what?' she asked coolly.

'The night we met you were smarting over your treatment at your defecting lover's hands.' His eyes locked with hers. 'Am I right?'

Joss nodded. 'Yes. You know that. Otherwise—'

Dan nodded swiftly. 'Otherwise you wouldn't have let me drive you home, let alone asked me to make love to you. Not,' he added, with a crooked smile, 'that I needed persuasion. But up to that point I'd actually deluded myself I could leave you on that bed and steal virtuously into the night.'

'I knew that all along. Which is why I was so shameless. But suddenly I needed my belief in myself as a woman restored.' She held his eyes. 'I'd never asked a man to make love to me before, and don't foresee doing it again. Ever.'

Dan nodded soberly. 'I realise that. But picture my feelings when I found you'd vanished. And the owner of your old flat flatly refused to give me your new address.'

'Nick was acting on instructions,' said Joss, biting her lip.

'Another slap in the face.' He took her hand. 'I came

back from my trip expecting to come courting, Joss—sounds naive now.'

'Not to me,' she said quietly.

'Then why the hell did you hide from me?'

'I was sure I'd be exchanging the frying pan for the fire. I gave you entirely the wrong impression about the real Joscelyn Hunter.' She gave him a wry smile. 'I may be a supposedly hard-nosed journalist, but underneath it all I'm still my father's daughter.'

'What was he like?' asked Dan with interest.

'Kind, humorous, supportive. Dad was the vicar of a large country parish in Warwickshire, and brought me up single-handed. My mother died when I was little.'

'So you're the product of lone parent upbringing, like Francis?'

Joss nodded. 'Mrs Herrick—Anna's mother—always treated me like a second daughter, but I used to envy girls who had mothers of their own. Which is part of the reason, in the end, why Peter Sadler left me.'

He frowned blankly. 'Run that past me again?'

'He wanted children right now. I didn't.'

'Why not?'

'I wanted to wait until our joint finances let me work from home. Being motherless myself, I was determined to be on hand for my child and do my job at the same time. The best of both worlds.' She eyed him challengingly. 'But, confidentially, I'm not sure I'm the maternal type. I don't drool over other people's babies. And I love my job the way it is. I was perfectly happy to wait.'

Dan nodded. 'I can appreciate that. Fatherhood doesn't appeal to me in the slightest. It does to Francis, but in his case it's only natural. He wants an heir for Eastlegh. But I applaud your honesty—Joss.' He smiled wryly.

'Your name doesn't exactly trip from the tongue yet. I still think of you as Eve.'

'You must have thought I was a total airhead, insisting on assumed names!'

He shook his head. 'I never doubted your intelligence. And *my* name wasn't assumed. I was christened Daniel Adam Francis Armstrong.'

'Of course—Adam after your great-grandfather. But why Francis?'

'All the first-born Morvilles are Francis. Old Lord Morville was my godfather, and insisted I took the name as well.'

'So you even share a name with Francis—did you cut each other's wrists and swear a blood oath, too?'

'Of course we did.' Dan nodded matter-of-factly, and held out a sinewy wrist where a slight scar was just visible. 'Before Francis went away to school.'

'Did you miss him when he went?'

'Damn right I did,' said Dan tersely. 'But to return to the subject of motherhood, did your lover jilt you for your lack of enthusiasm?'

Joss winced. 'It was part of it, I suppose. He'd been growing steadily more morose for weeks, which I took to be displeasure on the subject coupled with problems with his current project. But actually it was a lot more basic than that.' She shrugged. 'He just didn't want me anymore.'

'I do,' said Dan casually.

Joss sat very still, her heart thumping so loudly it seemed certain he could hear it.

'Did you hear what I said?'

'Yes.'

'You look stunned.'

'I feel stunned.'

'Why?' He leaned back, looking so relaxed Joss felt resentful.

'For one thing,' she began, pulling herself together, 'today, at lunch, you said you had no ambitions to fill the vacancy in my life.'

'I lied. I was still seething over your treatment, Miss Hunter.' He shrugged. 'I was furious when I came back from my travels to find you'd vanished.'

'I've explained about that.'

'Yes. Convinced I'd demand a repeat performance the moment I laid eyes on you.' He shook his head. 'Not likely, anyway, Joss. That kind of experience rarely happens twice.'

'True,' she said lightly, and got up. 'But I'm glad we did meet again.'

Dan rose slowly to his feet. 'Why?' he demanded.

'Because it gave me the opportunity to explain.' And because meeting him again made it plain her instincts had been faultless, after all.

'When I said that night could never be repeated,' Dan said deliberately, 'I meant the assumed names and the emotional state you were in.'

'I see.'

'I don't think you do.' Dan took her hand and drew her closer. 'I propose we backtrack a little. Get to know each other and go on from there.'

She looked at him steadily. 'That sounds very businesslike.'

'Then I'm putting on a good act.' His eyes glittered suddenly. 'To be blunt, I want to pick you up and take you to bed right now. But even if you were willing I wouldn't try.'

Joss stared at him, her eyes asking the question she couldn't bring herself to utter.

Dan smiled, and put out a hand to touch her cheek. 'If I did you'd be convinced that was all I wanted. And it isn't. Not by a long way.' He raised a sardonic eyebrow. 'Or is your opinion the same now we've seen each other in the light of day?'

'What opinion?'

'The one that sent you running for cover.'

'No,' she said honestly.

Dan frowned. 'Does that mean I pass muster after all, even now you know who I am?'

'Yes.'

'Does journalism train you to be monosyllabic?'

She scowled at him. 'It trains me in a lot of things, one of which is the ability to see both sides of an argument. Which means I can appreciate how you felt when I went missing. But try to put yourself in my shoes. My trust in men isn't exactly rock-solid these days.'

Dan looked at her levelly. 'You can trust *me*.'

Joss went over to her desk, took a snapshot from a drawer, and held it behind her back as she returned to him. 'If,' she began with care, 'we did become friends, is there anyone who might object to the arrangement?'

Dan frowned. 'A woman?'

For answer Joss held out the photograph of Dan at Ascot with his beautiful befeathered companion.

He took it, staring at it in surprise. 'Where did you get this?'

'I took it myself.'

'Then you *did* see me that day. Why the hell didn't you speak to me?' he demanded.

Joss shrugged. 'You were too involved with your companion.'

He tapped the photograph irritably. 'The Honourable Mrs Denby Hayter, to be precise. Otherwise Serena, cousin of our mutual friend Lord Morville, and incorrigible flirt all her life. Which is how long I've known her.' Dan advanced on her belligerently. 'So. Was Serena the reason for your second disappearing act?'

'Partly, yes.'

'Only part.' He seized her by the elbows, pulling her on tiptoe. 'Tell me. Was the other part because I disappointed you in bed?'

'No,' snapped Joss, trying to break free. 'You were wonderful, amazing, utterly unsurpassed in my experience—if you like I'll write a piece lauding your sexual prowess and publish it on the front page of the *Post*.'

For a moment Dan looked ready to shake her until her teeth rattled, then to Joss's relief he began to laugh and let her go.

'So you thought I was involved with Serena,' he said, grinning. 'Were you jealous?'

'Of course not,' she said scornfully. 'For all I knew the lady could have been your wife.'

'I told you I was unattached.'

'You wouldn't be the first to lie on the subject!'

'My father brought me up to tell the truth at all times,' said Dan virtuously, then his smile faded. 'It's getting late. I should go.'

Desperate for him to stay, Joss said the first thing that came into her head. 'Would you like a drink first?'

'No.' He moved closer. 'All I want is this.' He let out a deep, unsteady breath, then pulled her into his arms and kissed her mouth.

Joss didn't even try to resist. Whatever components made up Daniel Armstrong's chemical formula they reacted so instantly with her own that her response brought his arms round her like bands of steel.

'I didn't intend this,' he muttered against her mouth.

'You said that last time,' she muttered back.

'Then I won't talk any more!' Instead he kissed her with a demand her body welcomed with such ardour that Joss trembled in his arms, her tongue meeting his in an invitation he acknowledged by picking her up. 'Where's your bed?' he demanded hoarsely.

Joss stiffened. 'No!'

Dan set her on her feet so suddenly she staggered. They stood staring at each other, breath tearing through their chests.

'I apologise,' panted Dan raggedly.

Joss inclined her head in silent acknowledgement, unable to speak.

'And now, of course,' he said bitterly, 'you're convinced you were right.'

'No,' she said unsteadily. 'I know you didn't come here tonight just to—to—'

'Prove your suspicions correct.'

Joss smiled faintly. 'I was going to say to make love to me.'

'If,' he said tightly, 'we could talk about something else I might possibly stop wanting to do that.'

'Would you like a drink?' she said quickly.

His smile was wry. 'Black coffee?'

Joss went off to the kitchen alone, in desperate need of time to recover. What was it about this man? she thought despairingly. One touch of his hands and she melted like butter. And in a way she'd never been prone to before, with Peter or anyone else.

'Joss,' Dan said soberly, when she rejoined him. 'Let's start again.'

'Where, exactly?'

'From somewhere before I touched you.' His eyes met

hers. 'As must be painfully obvious, I can't allow myself to do that.'

She flushed, then busied herself with pouring coffee. 'Which is deeply flattering from my point of view. And reassuring.'

'Reassuring?'

'It convinces me I didn't go totally insane that night.' She handed him his coffee. 'But it does tend to make sensible conversation difficult.'

He grinned. 'At least you didn't throw me out.'

Joss looked him up and down. 'Somehow I can't see myself managing that single-handed. Besides...' She bit her lip.

'Besides what?' he prompted.

'I wasn't exactly fighting you off.'

'That honesty of yours again.'

She smiled wryly. 'Like you, I had early training in such matters.'

Dan drank his coffee quickly, then got to his feet. 'I'm off to Scotland in the morning, until Friday, unfortunately. But next Saturday I'll return your hospitality—on neutral territory. Just tell me which restaurant you prefer.'

'I haven't said I'm free next Saturday.'

Dan bent down to take her hand and pulled her to her feet. 'If you're not, cancel,' he ordered.

Her immediate instinct was to refuse. But some deep-hidden instinct responded quite shamelessly to such high-handedness. 'All right,' she said after a while.

'Where?' he demanded.

'I'll think about it—and fax my choice to you.'

Dan laughed, and raised her hand to his lips. 'This morning I had no idea what lay in store for me at Eastlegh.'

'Neither did I!' she said with feeling.

'If you had, would you have cancelled?'

'Certainly not. I was working, remember.' She looked up at him, very conscious of the hard hand still holding hers. 'How about you?'

'No way,' he said promptly, then spoilt it by reminding her that a visit to his parent had been his motive. 'Filial respect and all that,' he added virtuously.

Joss laughed, and tried to remove her hand, but Dan held onto it.

'I want to kiss you,' he said abruptly.

Because every one of her hormones was urging her to let him, Joss was well aware of it. 'Unwise,' she said reluctantly.

'And are you always wise?' he asked, his voice deepening to a note which dried her mouth.

'No,' she said unevenly. 'As you well know—' The rest of her words were smothered as his mouth made nonsense of her defences.

Joss gave herself up to the strength and barely controlled passion of his embrace, the heat and desire in his taut body arousing hers in a way no other man had ever been able to. Then she stopped thinking about other men, or about anything at all, as Dan sat her on the edge of the sofa and knelt between her parted knees to undo her shirt. With unsteady hands he freed her breasts to his lips and grazing teeth, stroking her covered thighs with caressing fingers which brought her rapidly to an arousal equal to his own. This time there was no mention of bed. By unspoken consent they sank to the floor, upsetting the coffee tray with a crash neither of them even noticed in their frantic haste to shed each other's clothes, their wild caresses rousing each other to such a state of frenzy their mating was short, but shatteringly sweet, the magic as powerful as before.

Afterwards, it was a long time before either of them stirred. Dan raised his head at last and looked down at Joss's flushed face and kissed the beads of moisture away from her upper lip.

'You're a dangerous lady,' he said hoarsely. 'I've never lost it like that before.'

Joss opened a considering eye. 'Tactless to mention "before" right now,' she pointed out, and Dan grinned.

'Point taken.' His grin widened as he spotted various garments scattered among broken china and spilt sugar from the coffee tray. 'Not that I've ever been in this particular situation with a woman before.'

Joss detached herself sufficiently to look and shuddered. 'What a *mess*!' She struggled to get up but Dan prevented her, looking down at her in a way which drove all thoughts of clearing up from her mind.

'Are you going to make love to me again?' she asked bluntly.

Dan's silent laugh vibrated against her breasts. 'Since you ask, yes. Why?'

'This floor is hard.'

'When I asked about bed last time it put an end to proceedings,' he reminded her, his lazy, skilful hands making sure this was unlikely a second time.

'My bedroom's at the end of the hall,' gasped Joss, and Dan pulled her to her feet, kissed her, then scooped her up in his arms and carried her to bed.

It was the early hours of morning before Dan forced himself to break away. 'I must get home,' he said without enthusiasm. 'I haven't even packed yet.'

'Do you want a shower before you go?' said Joss, yawning, then raised an eyebrow at the sudden gleam in his eyes. 'What?'

'Have one with me,' he said, kissing a bare toe.

The shower took a long time, and ended in more love-making and then another shower, so that dawn had over-taken them before Dan was finally ready to go.

'This time,' he said sternly, from the foot of the bed, 'don't steal away in the morning without telling me.'

Joss shook her head, and pulled the covers up to her chin. 'Nowhere to go.'

Dan took a wallet from his back pocket and fished out a card. 'You can reach me at either number if you need me.'

Joss took the card and held it to the lamp to read it, her face suddenly blank with astonishment. 'Is *this* your company?'

'Yes. It's relatively small as yet, but expanding fast. I promise you, Athena will soon be one of the biggest names in property development. Why do you ask?'

Joss gave him a very odd little smile. 'Peter Sadler's an architect. He worked for one of the firms who tendered for your riverside development. You turned his plans down.'

Dan eyed her challengingly. 'Does it make a differ-ence?'

'To what, exactly?'

'To a relationship between us.' He strode round the bed to sit beside her.

Joss shook her head. 'Why should it? You chose the best tender for the job; Peter's effort didn't come up to scratch. End of story.'

Dan took her in his arms and held her close. 'No,' he said against her hair. 'Not the end. For us it's just begin-ning.' He put her away from him and looked down into her flushed face. 'Though if I'd met you beforehand I'd have thrown Sadler's plans out without looking at them.

He had his chance with you and blew it. Do you still mind about that?'

Joss considered for a moment, then answered with her usual candour. 'No. Not after meeting up with you again.'

Dan smoothed her hair back from her face. 'In that case, Miss Hunter, am I going too fast if I demand exclusive rights on your free time from now on?'

Joss looked at him thoughtfully. 'I enjoy socialising with other journalists—male and female—for a meal or a drink after work sometimes.'

'Done,' he said promptly. 'But keep the male company in the plural.'

'And I work very irregular hours,' she reminded him. 'With Peter that was always a bone of contention. I can never guarantee to be in the right place at the right time.'

'Neither can I,' he said, then took her breath away. 'Move in with me, Joss. That way we can at least spend whatever free time we've got together.'

Joss shook her head firmly. 'It's too soon for that, Dan. I'm still recovering from my last relationship. Let's get to know each other better first. For the moment I rather like living alone again.'

Dan looked down at her in silence, then a wry smile curved his mouth. 'It can't be soon enough for me, but I'll wait—but only for a while, Joss. On the journey to Scotland I'll think up ways to make you change your mind.'

'Have you lived with a woman before?' she asked bluntly.

'No. Unless you count a flat shared with both sexes in my student days.' Dan shrugged. 'But that was just accommodation. You're the first woman I've asked to share on a one-to-one basis.'

'Really?' She wreathed her hands behind his head,

bringing his mouth to hers for a kiss that quickly threatened to get out of hand again.

'If I don't go now,' said Dan thickly, 'I'll miss the plane.' He straightened, his smile crooked as he looked down at her. 'I'll give you breathing space, Joscelyn Hunter. But not much. Why waste time apart when we could be together?'

CHAPTER SIX

WHILE Dan was away on his travels Joss threw herself into her work with a zest which had been missing since Peter's departure. Colleagues noticed, and teased, but Joss refused to give details. For the moment her new, fledgling relationship with Daniel Armstrong was a secret she hugged to herself, unable to discuss it with anyone except Anna, who approved heartily, particularly since Dan was a friend of a friend of Hugh.

Until her broken engagement Joss had been utterly sure of her goals in life, confident that she was liked and even respected by her colleagues, and loved by Peter Sadler. But she had been wrong about the last, and in the recesses of her mind a little seed of insecurity refused to wither and die. Until she was officially living with Dan Armstrong she would keep their relationship private. But in the meantime, when her training overcame her reluctance to pry, she did some in-depth research on the man who'd made such a success of Athena.

Because Daniel Armstrong shunned publicity, Joss discovered little more about him than she already knew, other than his phenomenal success. She read a lot about his aim to provide buildings which blended with their environment, but the only photographs were shots of Dan at race-meetings, or in the financial section, with none of him on the town with beautiful women. Dan had obviously been truthful when he'd told her he was no party animal.

To her great satisfaction Dan rang Joss every night,

and always ended the conversation by reminding her that her breathing space was one day less.

'Have you missed me?' he demanded, towards the end of the week.

'Yes.'

'How much?'

'A lot. Yet this time last week I thought we'd never meet again.'

'That, Joscelyn Hunter, was never a possibility. I would have found you eventually, even if I'd had to hire someone to do it for me.'

'Would you really have done that?'

'Damn right I would.'

She paused. 'Was it just because we were so good in bed together?'

Dan's chuckle sent the familiar trickle down her spine. 'I would be lying if I said it wasn't part of it, but there's a whole lot more than that. So get yourself in the mood to move as quickly as you can. Patience isn't my strongest point.'

The week was a particularly busy one, for which Joss was grateful. Even so the days seemed to go by far more slowly than usual, and Saturday refused to come quickly. It was useless to tell herself to stop it, that she was a mature, level-headed woman. One, moreover, who only recently had expected to marry Peter Sadler. Was this purely a rebound thing? On Friday night Joss shook her head at her reflection in the mirror. If she were totally honest—and it was her honesty that Dan particularly admired—it was a good thing she hadn't met him before Peter's departure. Otherwise she might have been the one who'd left Peter, rather than the other way round. Shaken by this discovery, Joss faced the truth. The persistence which she brought both to her job and her private life

had made her fight to keep her relationship with Peter
alive long after it had shown unmistakable signs of fal-
tering. When Peter finally left her pride had taken the
beating, not her heart.

Joss took a quick shower and went to bed early with
a book, too restless to watch television. But instead of
reading she kept scowling at the telephone beside her
bed, willing it to ring. She stretched out in the bed, clasp-
ing her hands behind her head, and stared at the ceiling.
Living alone had lost its attraction very quickly. Dan's
fault entirely. He was such a big man in every way that
his absence left a space impossible to fill. But moving in
with him was a risky proposition. Relationships changed.
As she knew. After a while Dan might want out, just as
Peter had. She'd known Peter for years, and her time with
Dan could be measured in hours, but she had a strong
suspicion that recovering from a break-up with Dan
would be a lot less easy. Maybe not even possible.

Joss gave up trying to sleep in favour of tea and a
book. When she was on her way to the kitchen the doorbell rang, and her heart leapt. Joss ran to the door, picked
up the receiver and spoke into it, her heart thudding as
she heard Dan's voice.

'I couldn't wait until tomorrow,' he said tersely.

Joss pressed the buzzer for answer, and a minute later
Dan came bounding up the stairs to snatch her up into
his arms and kiss her until her head was reeling. When
he released her at last, he grinned down at her striped
nightshirt. 'So that's what you wear to bed.'

Joss laughed, secretly glorying in his impatience to see
her. 'You mean you came round here at this time of night
just to find out what I wear to bed?'

'No. I came,' he said very deliberately, 'because I
couldn't wait another minute to hold you in my arms.'

'Good,' said Joss, her matter-of-fact tone at odds with the tattoo her heart was beating under the cotton. 'Are you hungry?'

Dan picked her up and sat down on the sofa, settling her comfortably on his lap. 'Not for food. I ate on the plane.' He smoothed her head against his shoulder and let out a deep sigh of satisfaction. 'So, tell me about your week, Miss Hot-Shot Journalist.'

Joss obliged, telling him about the various assignments she'd been given, of the photographs taken at Eastlegh, and, in the end, confessed that she'd done some research into the career of Daniel Armstrong, founder of Athena Developments. She raised her face to look at him. 'Do you mind?'

He shook his head. 'No. Because you told me about it. The women in my past rarely considered candour important. You, my darling, are different.'

Elated by the endearment, Joss ran a hand along his jaw. 'You need a shave,' she said huskily.

'I need a lot of things,' he said, grinning down at her.

She frowned at him in mock disapproval. 'You might have rung first. I could have had a visitor.'

Dan's eyes narrowed menacingly. 'Another man?'

'Of course not! I was thinking of Anna. Or I could have been hosting the occasional get-together with some fellow journalists—female variety.' Joss freed herself from his arms and sat upright, her eyes steady on his. 'Listen, Dan. There were men in my life before Peter Sadler. But only one at a time. And no one since. Except you. I thought you might have taken that for granted after—after last weekend.'

'Pax!' Dan pulled her down into his arms, rubbing his cheek against her hair. 'I apologise—humbly.'

'You, *humble*?' Joss snorted inelegantly.

'Yes,' he said flatly. 'I never knew what jealousy meant before you, Joss. All the time I was trying to bring canny, hard-headed Scots round to my way of thinking I kept wondering what you were doing, and who you were doing it with. Your face kept getting between me and the matter in hand.'

'I'm flattered.' Joss slid her arms round him under his jacket. 'But bear with me, Dan. Let's go on seeing each other for a while before I burn my boats.'

Dan tipped her face up to his. 'Don't you fancy living with me?'

'Of course I do. A lot. But I'm not normally the type to throw caution to the winds. Nor,' she added, 'are you the type of man to respect me if I did.'

'True,' he conceded. 'All right. You win. I won't push. For the moment, anyway. So where do you want to go tomorrow?'

'The forecast is good.' Joss smiled at him coaxingly. 'Could we just go somewhere and walk in the fresh air?'

'No restaurants or smart nightspots?' he mocked, tracing a fingertip over her bottom lip. 'A pearl among women!'

'You don't care for that kind of thing, according to my research.'

'I don't. I would very much enjoy walking with you.' He looked at her for a moment. 'I live near Kew Gardens. We can walk there, then I could feed you at my place afterwards. Perhaps it might tempt you to move sooner.'

Joss nodded. 'Sounds good. I'd like that.'

'Done,' said Dan, and yawned widely. 'Sorry.' He stood up with her in his arms, then set her on her feet. 'Time I was off.'

She stared at him blankly.

He smiled. 'You obviously thought I meant to stay the

night. Which, of course, I would very much prefer to driving back to Kew. For obvious reasons. But if I stay you'll be convinced that bed was all I came for. And it wasn't.'

Joss was assailed by a variety of emotions, elation and disappointment battling for supremacy as she followed Dan down to the door. At the foot of the stairs he took her in his arms and kissed her.

'Sleep well. I'll collect you in the morning.'

'But I can drive myself to Kew—'

'No. I'll come for you,' he said flatly, then kissed her again. 'Aren't you proud of me?' he said against her lips. 'Awestruck by my restraint?'

'Absolutely,' she agreed, and kissed him lingeringly to show her admiration.

'That's not fair,' Dan said hoarsely, but he kissed her again at length before he finally made it through the door, leaving Joss to wander back upstairs in a daze of happiness.

That night marked the beginning of a relationship which very swiftly became such a vital part of Joss's life it effectively blotted out her time with Peter Sadler. Sometimes it was hard to remember she'd shared her life with anyone other than Daniel Adam Francis Armstrong. They saw each other as much as their various lifestyles allowed, and when Joss was obliged to cancel at the last minute, due to the demands of her job, the only objections raised by Dan were his opposition to her continued residence in Acton.

'I'm tired of having you with me in small doses,' he said, late one hot, starlit Sunday night. 'If you lived here we would at least come home to each other. Actual time spent together is a very small percentage of our acquaintance, Miss Hunter. Too damn small. I want more. A lot more.'

They were lying together on a wicker chaise longue in the walled courtyard behind Dan's home in Kew. The house was large and very private behind tall, dense hedges in a quiet side-road that could have been in the country instead of near the famous gardens. Joss adored everything about the house. She had been trying to bring herself to leave for the past half-hour, knowing what Dan's reaction would be. Every time they parted his arguments grew more persuasive.

'I'll put the flat on the market tomorrow,' she said suddenly, and said no more for some time as Dan seized her in his arms and kissed her by way of demonstrating his triumph at her surrender.

'You mean that?' he said eventually.

Joss nodded, too breathless even to say yes.

'Why now?' he demanded. 'I've been persuading—'

'Bullying,' she corrected.

'I've been persuading you for weeks,' he went on, shaking her slightly. 'What's so special about tonight?'

'Because in a minute I've got to drive back to Acton, and I don't want to.'

'At last,' he said smugly. 'The lady admits she hates the thought of leaving me.'

'Oh, it's not you,' lied Joss shamelessly. 'It's the house.'

'Witch!' His voice deepened to the note which always melted her bones. 'As long as you come and share it with me I'll try not to be jealous of it.' He laughed. 'Listen to me! I never imagined a woman lived who could change me so much.' He tipped her face up to his. 'Tell me the truth. Were you jealous when you saw me with Serena at Ascot?'

'Horribly. Which is why I ran away. I couldn't bear the sight of you together.'

Dan kissed her hard by way of appreciation. 'As a matter of interest, did you feel jealous where Sadler was concerned?'

Joss thought about it for a moment. 'No,' she said, surprised. 'Never. Nor about anyone else, either. I've always disapproved of jealousy.'

'Including mine?'

'No.' She smiled up at him. 'I like that a lot. Very ego-boosting.'

He laughed, and pulled her bodily into his lap. 'I know other ways to boost your ego. Want me to demonstrate?'

'No,' she said firmly. 'Otherwise I'll never leave.'

'I know!'

'Dan, please, I've got work tomorrow; it's time I went—' Joss stopped mid-sentence. 'I was going to say time I went home,' she said, looking up into his eyes. 'But from the day you brought me here your house feels like home. Not the flat.'

'Then move in with me tomorrow,' he said urgently. 'To hell with the flat. Let an estate agent sell it for you.'

Joss was sorely tempted, but in the end she shook her head. 'Don't be angry with me, Dan, but I'd like to stay there until it's sold. Organise it myself. I need to be in control of my own life. It's a big step from living alone to dependence on you for the roof over my head.'

Dan looked down at her in silence for a moment. 'Joss,' he said slowly, 'it's a house, not a cage. And you'll have your own key. And live your life the way you want to. The only difference will be sharing your spare time, and my bed, with me. I did mention that bed was part of the arrangement?' he added.

'Why else do you think I'm moving in?' she said, smiling provocatively as she jumped up.

He leapt to his feet and took her in his arms, laughing. 'Do I take that as a compliment?'

'You certainly do,' she assured him, and held up her face for his kiss.

For the next week Joss spent any spare time left over from Dan and her job in cleaning and polishing the flat to maximum allure for potential buyers. The estate agent she contacted was optimistic about a quick sale, and, having burnt her boats, Joss called Anna to tell her about the move.

'Well, hello,' said Anna, when Joss rang. 'I thought maybe you'd emigrated.'

'Sorry, love. I've been a bit busy lately.'

'This Dan of yours must be really something. Bring him down to see us so the Herricks—and Hugh, of course—can make sure he's good enough for you.'

'Sorry,' said Joss, laughing. 'It's too late for that.'

'Why?'

'For your ears only, Anna, I'm head over heels in love with him,' Joss blurted, putting the truth into words for the first time. 'In fact the moment I've sold the flat I'm moving into his house in Kew.'

'I thought you might,' said Anna jubilantly. 'Oh, Joss, I'm so happy for you. And very glad you've recovered from Peter. By the way, I met him outside his father's office in Stratford the other day.'

'How was he?'

'Very much on the defensive with me, as usual. But he asked about you, so I took great pleasure in telling him about your relationship with Dan Armstrong. But never mind Peter. Come down to lunch one Sunday.

Mother misses you. So do I. Bring Daniel to the lions' den. We won't eat him.'

'You couldn't,' chuckled Joss. 'He's too big.'

'Seriously, Joss, we'd love to see you. Will he come?'

'I'll ask him, and let you know. But thank your mother for me and give her my love, your father, too. And tell Hugh the article on Eastlegh Hall was a great success. Lord Morville—Francis—is a charmer.'

'So Hugh says. But if your Dan is a friend of his, how come Hugh doesn't know him?'

Joss explained, promised to drive down to Warwickshire with Dan as soon as possible, then rang off and took advantage of a rare early night alone.

Because Dan was tied up with problems about his riverside complex Joss showed several people round the immaculate flat during mid-week evenings. Afterwards the agent told her there was a lot of interest in the property, but she could sell it at once if she were willing to drop the price a trifle. Joss wouldn't hear of it. She wanted the full asking price as a nest-egg, and eventually one of the prospective purchasers agreed to pay the full amount as long as they could move in as soon as possible.

'I've done it!' said Joss in triumph when Dan rang later that night. 'I've sold the flat.'

'Already?' He whistled. 'Did you give way on the price?'

'No way.'

'Good! So when are you moving in with me?'

'As soon as I exchange contracts,' she promised. 'The purchasers want immediate possession.'

'So do I!' he said, the note in his voice as tactile as a caress.

'I'll drive to Kew as early as I can on Friday evening,' she promised breathlessly.

'That's forty-eight hours away,' he said gloomily. 'I hate Thursdays.'

'Since I met you I'm not keen on them either, but it's my job, Dan.'

'I know, I know. Make sure you get off early on Friday.' His voice deepened. 'I'm impatient to have you here with me all the time.'

'I'll still have to work late.'

'But afterwards you'll come home to me, my darling.'

Joss went to bed smiling, her happiness complete except for one tiny flaw. Dan made it very plain at all times that he respected her intelligence, and liked being with her whatever they were doing, quite apart from their physical rapport and the shameless amount of time they spent in bed. But he'd never said a word about love. He just found it hard to express his feelings, she assured herself. She could understand that. Up to now she'd been the same. But recently it had taken every ounce of self-control she possessed not to express her own feelings when they made love.

Thursday was even more hectic than usual, and it was very late by the time Joss got back to Acton. She unlocked the door and climbed the stairs wearily, longing for a hot bath and some beauty sleep in preparation for seeing Dan next day. While she was exchanging her clothes for a towelling robe the doorbell rang, and she smiled radiantly, forgetting her fatigue. So Dan hadn't been able to wait after all. She ran to lift the receiver.

'Impatient man!' she said lovingly. 'Come up.'

But the man who came through the door at the foot of the stairs was slim and fair, and half the size of Daniel Armstrong. As he ran up towards her the triumphant smile on Peter Sadler's face made Joss want to slap it.

'What are you doing here?' she said furiously. 'How did you find out my address?'

'I met Anna recently. She let slip that you lived in Acton, and because the Holts now live in our place I made an educated guess,' he said airily.

'I'm sorry you went to the trouble,' she said curtly, 'because you can't stay. I'm tired and I want to get to bed.'

He pushed back a lock of fair hair, eyeing her narrowly. 'You've changed, Joss. You've grown hard.'

She stood with arms folded, her eyes implacable on his fair, good-looking face, secretly astonished that she'd once imagined her happiness depended on him.

'I would have got in touch before, but you wouldn't answer my messages,' he said, moving nearer. 'When you wrote you didn't give your address, so I couldn't even thank you for sending the furniture back, or the cheque.'

'If you've come to do that now, fine,' snapped Joss. 'But right now I need to get to bed.'

'Not yet. Joss, listen to me. I made a mistake,' he said, astonishing her. 'I want you back.'

She stared at him blankly. 'You must be joking!'

Peter's eyes narrowed dangerously. 'Not a thing to joke about. After the Athena rejection things got out of proportion for a while. But I've had time to reconsider—'

'So have I,' said Joss quickly. 'And you were right, Peter. I have changed. When you left I made a new life. And I much prefer it to the old one. There's no place in it for you.'

His eyes narrowed in sudden malevolence. 'So you're telling me you feel nothing for me?'

'You did a great hatchet job on my feelings,' she reminded him coldly. 'Now I think of you—when I think of you at all—as part of a growing-up process.'

'I'd hardly describe it like that, Joss,' he sneered. 'You're thirty-two years old.'

'True,' she said unmoved. 'I wasted a lot of time on you.'

Peter moved like lightning, seizing her by the elbows. 'I could *make* you want me again!'

'Oh, *please*,' said Joss, deliberately bored—something she regretted as Peter dragged her close with a show of strength which took her by surprise. He ground his mouth against hers and, enraged, Joss tried to break free. But one of Peter's stylish boots landed on her bare foot, and she let out a choked cry of pain as they collapsed on the sofa in a writhing mass of arms and legs. Peter Sadler was slim, but wiry, and in his present mood Joss found she was no match for him. He flattened himself on top of her, one hand cruelly tight in her hair as he smothered her protests with his mouth, the other pushing the robe away to get at her breasts. Joss shuddered with distaste, bracing herself to break free. Then Peter raised his head and smiled in pure triumph, and she gave a gasp of horror as she saw Dan at the head of the stairs, staring at them in disbelief. Joss clutched her robe together, reaching out a hand in entreaty, but with a look which stabbed her to the heart Dan turned his back and left as silently as he'd arrived.

Peter got to his feet at once, holding out his hand to Joss as politely as though the assault of a minute before had never happened.

'Get out!' she spat.

'Certainly,' he said, smoothing his hair. 'Sorry I was rough.'

'I should call the police,' she said bitterly.

'Not much point in that, Joss.' He smiled blandly. 'I didn't rape you.'

Joss shook with rage, wanting to throw him out bodily so she could run after Dan. But Dan, she realised hopelessly, would be well on his way to Kew by now.

'*Why*, Peter?' she flung at him, tightening the belt on her robe.

'I had my reasons,' he said enigmatically, and looked at his watch. 'From a personal point of view my visit has been a great success. But time I was off.' He went to the head of the stairs, then gave her a smile which clenched her hands into claws. 'I'm so sorry your visitor got the wrong impression.'

'No, you're not,' Joss stalked towards him with menace, feeling fierce satisfaction as he backed away, the smile suddenly wiped from his face. 'Get out of my life, Peter. And this time stay out.'

Peter looked at her for a moment, opened his mouth to say something, then thought better of it as he met the look in her eyes, and ran downstairs without a word. After the door had clicked shut behind him Joss felt cold with reaction. Shivering, she clutched her arms across her chest, eyeing the phone with longing. But Dan wouldn't be home yet. And what she had to say was impossible to leave as a message. To pass the time, and get warm again, she soaked in a bath as hot as she could bear, desperate to remove the soiled feeling left by Peter's hands. The hands whose caresses she had once welcomed. Joss ground her teeth in angry frustration, able to recognise, now she had time to think, that Peter's assault had been punitive, and nothing at all to do with love, or even sex. But why was he punishing her? He was the one who'd walked out.

Joss ran water over her head for a long time in the

urge to feel clean, but at last swathed a towel round her head, wrapped herself in another, then went to the phone to ring Dan and found the red light glowing. She pressed the button, then stood in disbelief, listening to the message Dan had left while she'd washed her hair.

'I'm glad you're not there,' he said, in a tone which tore her to pieces. 'If you intended ringing me with explanations, don't. It's finished between us. Nothing you can say will make any difference.'

Joss rang his number just the same, convinced that she could make him understand if he'd only listen. But the only response was his recorded message.

'Dan, pick up the phone,' she said unevenly. 'Please listen to me. I can explain. *Please!*' She rang again, several times during the next hour, and at last, disgusted with herself for pleading, Joss gave up and went to bed, to lie awake in dry-eyed misery too intense for tears.

Early next morning Joss rang Dan again, but with the same result. Then she rang his office, and was told by his personal assistant that Mr Armstrong had given instructions that he was unavailable to Miss Hunter, or any other reporter. At least, she thought dully, he'd added the face-saving bit about reporters. After an hour of coming to terms with unwelcome reality, Joss rang the estate agent and told him she no longer wished to sell. And at work, when told she looked like death, she lied about an oncoming cold and got through the day as best she could.

When she got home she rang Anna, to say, as flippantly as possible, that she wouldn't be bringing Dan down after all, but if the Herricks would put up with a very depressed guest, she would take them up on their offer of Sunday lunch.

'Dan walked out on me,' Joss said baldly.

'Oh, Joss, no!' said Anna, horrified. 'Drive down in

the morning and stay the weekend. Hugh's gone off on a cricket tour, so come and be cosseted.'

At first Joss demurred, unable to quench a little flicker of hope that Dan might have a change of heart and contact her. But in the end she accepted Anna's invitation, grateful for an alternative to a weekend spent alone in the flat. Only a short time ago she'd expected to spend it in Dan's company, in Dan's arms, in Dan's bed. Something which, he'd made very clear, would never happen again.

CHAPTER SEVEN

Joss felt her heart lift when she saw Anna, clad in the inevitable jodhpurs and riding boots, wild dark hair blowing in the breeze as she came running from the open door of Glebe House.

'I took Goodfellow out for a ride first thing,' said Anna. 'Haven't had time to change.' She hugged Joss close, then held her at arm's length. 'Heavens, you look ghastly. Mother and Dad have tactfully taken themselves off to a flower show, so we're on our own for a bit. You can cry as much as you like.'

'No crying,' said Joss firmly, returning the hug.

'Want to tell me about it?' said Anna as they went inside. 'We'll have lunch first; you can take your things upstairs later.'

The big kitchen, with its old-fashioned cupboards and big square table, was so hearteningly familiar and unchanged that Joss gave a sigh of pleasure. 'It's so good to be here. Thanks for letting me come.'

Anna gave her a withering look as she took a napkin from a plate of sandwiches. 'It wasn't a case of "letting," Joss. I've been trying to get you down here for ages. I only wish it had been under happier circumstances. Come on, sit down. Do you want tea, coffee, or something alcoholic and mind-numbing?'

Joss grinned. 'Tea. I draw the line at breathing gin fumes over your mother.'

'That's better,' approved Anna as she made tea. 'Nice to see you can still smile.' She sat down and fixed Joss with a commanding hazel eye. 'Right. Tell me what happened.'

Joss gave a short, succinct account of Peter's visit, and apart from the odd exclamation Anna managed to keep from interrupting until the end.

'You should have reported him to the police,' she said, and bit into a sandwich as though it were Peter Sadler's jugular.

'What could I have said?' said Joss. 'He didn't rape me—in fact, looking back on it, I know he never intended that. He just wanted to frighten and humiliate me, for some reason. Which is rich. He was the one who walked out.'

'Hmm,' said Anna, unconvinced. 'Couldn't you have charged him with bodily harm, or something?'

'The harm he did wasn't physical,' said Joss bitterly.

'But surely if you explained to Dan Armstrong he'd believe you?'

'He wouldn't answer the phone at home, and when I rang his office his secretary told me he was permanently unavailable to Miss Hunter.'

'Ouch!' said Anna, and nudged the plate of sandwiches nearer. 'Eat one. Just to please me,' she coaxed.

Joss did her best, but the food stuck in her throat. 'I just don't seem to feel hungry lately,' she said apologetically.

'No wonder!' Anna poured tea, and handed a cup to Joss. 'You haven't known this Dan Armstrong long,' she went on. 'Will it be very hard to get over him?'

'At the moment it seems impossible. But I'll do it. Eventually.' Joss managed a smile. 'Journalists are persistent beasts, remember?'

Her friend eyed her thoughtfully. 'Have you given up all idea of knocking the truth into the man's head?'

Joss lifted her chin belligerently. 'I did my bit of pleading, Anna, and hated it. No way am I doing it again.'

The weekend with the Herricks did Joss a lot of good. She was able to face work with more zest the following week, even though it became obvious, as days went by, that Dan had meant what he said. With all hope finally quenched, Joss buckled down to reshaping her life, and because it was holiday season there was no shortage of work to pass the time. In the evenings she reverted to having a meal after work with other journalists, and sometimes went on to a film or the theatre, no matter how tired she was. And the dreaded *longueurs* of the weekends were filled by sub-editing work for whichever Sunday paper required her services.

Some nights she fell into bed too exhausted even to mourn her ill-fated passion for Dan Armstrong. Because passion, she assured herself bitterly, was all it had been. She had been—and still was—deeply in love with him, but on Dan's side the relationship had obviously been purely physical. But she was no teenager, mourning the death of calf-love. She was thirty-two years old, with sufficient maturity to prevent Daniel Adam Francis Armstrong from ruining her life. He had spoiled her for the company of other men, it was true. But that would pass. Time, and her own determination, would make sure it did. But her fine resolutions failed to damp down the rush of hope every time her phone rang. Or to prevent intense disappointment when her caller was never Dan.

To Joss's surprise Francis Legh rang her one evening, to tell her he was bringing Sarah Wilcox up to an auction next day and wondered if Joss could spare an hour to have lunch with them. She made a hasty mental rear-

rangement of her itinerary for the next day and accepted
with pleasure.

'I know that something went wrong between you and
Dan.' Francis went on, startling her. 'If you'd rather we
didn't mention him we won't.'

'It makes no difference to me,' she lied airily.

'Really?'

Joss sighed. 'No, *not* really. Not yet, anyway. But I'm
working on it. Thank you for the invitation, Francis, but
bear with me if I'm not punctual to the minute.'

Joss looked thoughtful after she'd put the phone down.
Lord Morville was a very subtle man, she decided. With
Sarah along there was no ambiguity about his invitation—or his intention. Not that she had any aspirations
where Francis was concerned. He was charming, friendly,
good-looking in a well-bred kind of way, but though she
liked him very much he paled into insignificance com-
pared with Dan. In which case, Joss told herself vi-
ciously, it was time to stop comparing men with Dan
Armstrong and from now on just view them on their own
merits.

Next day it was hot and sunny, and Joss wore a dress
bought to celebrate moving in with Dan. Sleeveless, V-
necked, in a powder-pink knitted fabric fragile as cob-
webs, the dress clung rather more than she'd remembered, but it was flattering and she felt good in it as she
walked into the restaurant she'd read so much about in
the reviews. At the mention of Lord Morville Joss was
ushered to a table where Francis jumped up, hand outstretched, as she approached.

'Joss, you made it.'

To her surprise he kissed her on both cheeks, then
turned to the young woman smiling at them from a chair
by the window.

'You remember Joss, darling?'

'Hello,' said Sarah Wilcox warmly. 'Nice to see you again.'

Joss took the chair Francis held out for her, and after conventional greetings looked from one face to the other with a questioning smile. 'Is there something a journalist should know? Or are the hearts and flowers strictly off the record?'

'Off the record, for the time being,' said Sarah, flushing.

'Haven't asked her father yet,' said Francis, beckoning the wine waiter.

'So why am I playing gooseberry?' asked Joss.

'I proposed on the way up in the train this morning,' said Francis, grinning. 'No one knows yet—I haven't even given Sarah a ring—' He broke off to go into a discussion about the choice of wine, and when menus were put in front of them sat back in his seat, looking very pleased with himself.

'Congratulations to you both,' said Joss sincerely, quelling a dart of pain. 'I hope—no, I *know* you'll be very happy.'

'Thank you,' said Sarah, and gave her a very straight look. 'Something tells me you're not surprised.'

Joss tapped her nose. 'My instincts are rarely wrong. I suspected as much the day I visited Eastlegh.'

'Talking of which, Sam Armstrong took quite a fancy to you,' said Francis. 'He approved of the article you wrote. So do I—heartily. Business is twice as brisk since it appeared. This lunch is by way of a small token of appreciation.'

'That's very nice of you.' Joss smiled warmly. 'The photographs turned out so well my editor decided on Eastlegh as the main thrust of the article.'

Francis had placed her with her back to the room. When Sarah looked up with a smile of welcome a few minutes later Joss felt the hairs rise on the back of her neck, like an animal scenting danger.

Francis sprang to his feet, hand outstretched. 'Hello, Dan, better late than never. Help us celebrate.'

For a moment time seemed suspended. Dan took one look at Joss and obviously wanted to turn on his heel and walk out. But good manners and his genuine attachment to Francis and Sarah prevailed. He took his friend's hand and shook it, eyeing him in enquiry.

'Celebrate?'

'I've just persuaded Sarah to marry me. And I've sold another manorial title.'

Because every nerve in Joss's body was hypersensitive to Dan's slightest reaction she could have sworn that his first gut reaction was relief. Then he went round the table to kiss Sarah, and at last greeted Joss, with a courtesy which chilled her to the bone.

To the onlooker it was an ordinary lunch party, with four people enjoying the food and each other's company, but to Joss it was a particularly refined form of torture. Not by a flicker of an eyelash did Dan portray the slightest hostility towards her. He was, if anything, far more pleasant to her than on the day at Eastlegh. Yet the experience was worse. Sheer determination made Joss eat some of the exquisite food and drink a sip or two of the celebratory champagne. But Dan said nothing directly to Joss, nor she to him, and only Francis's skill as a host kept the conversational ball in the air as he discussed plans for a party at Eastlegh to celebrate the engagement in proper style.

'You'll come, Joss, of course,' he said.

'Thank you,' she said, surprised. 'I'll look forward to it.'

'You too, Dan,' said Francis, and gave his friend a straight look. 'Wasn't it on a similar occasion that you met Joss?'

'Yes, it was,' said Dan briefly, and changed the subject. 'So which of your extraneous titles did you sell off today?'

'I've heard about this,' said Joss, her interest caught. 'Was that the auction you came up for?'

Sarah nodded. 'Quite a few manorial titles went under the hammer today. Ours did particularly well,' she added, eyes sparkling. 'Every time the price went up I totted up more lead for the Eastlegh roof.'

'That's my girl,' said Francis lovingly, and raised the hand he held to his lips.

'What did you do with the money I paid for mine?' said Dan.

Joss stared at him. Daniel Armstrong had actually paid money to Francis so he could add Lord of some Manor to his credentials? In her astonishment she barely heard Francis talking about unromantic plumbing repairs. Dan caught the look in her eye and smiled sardonically.

'Thinking up a new headline, Joss? ''Gardener's son aspires to Lord of the Manor status''?'

She shook her head. 'One of my colleagues followed the sale of manorial titles some time ago.'

'But I didn't feature in it,' he pointed out. 'No one knows about mine.'

'Nor would have done today, if you hadn't mentioned it,' said Francis, eyeing him narrowly.

Dan shrugged. 'It's not a dark secret.'

'Well, no but—'

'As Joss says,' interrupted Dan firmly, 'it's old news.'

Joss got up, looking pointedly at her watch, and the men rose with her. 'Talking of news, I'd better get back to it. Thursday's a busy day for me.' She noted a pulse throbbing at the corner of Dan's mouth, and rejoiced. Mention of Thursday had struck a chord his impervious mask couldn't hide.

'It's time we were all away,' said Francis, helping Sarah from her chair, and to Joss's dismay the four of them left the restaurant together. She had desperately wanted to leave first, and leave alone at that, due to an unpleasant feeling she put down to an overdose of stress.

'Can we give you a lift, Joss?' said Sarah.

To Joss, the heat of the day seemed intense after the cool room inside. She shook her head, meaning to say something about a taxi, then gasped as the earth shifted beneath her feet. Great spots of light danced in front of her eyes, and Dan leapt to catch her as she fell.

When Joss came to she was lying on a sofa in the restaurant's powder room, with Sarah bending over her anxiously.

'How do you feel?'

'What happened?' Joss struggled to sit up and Sarah sat beside her, supporting her with a comforting arm.

'You fainted.'

Joss groaned. 'I never faint! I hardly drank anything, either.'

'I know. Maybe it was something you ate. Drink this.' Sarah handed her a glass of water and Joss drank thirstily, then gave Sarah a rueful smile.

'Sorry I messed up your celebration.'

'You didn't,' said Sarah firmly, and smiled. 'Nothing could do that.'

'You really love Francis, don't you?' said Joss, mopping her forehead with the tissue Sarah gave her.

'From the moment I first saw him, though he never seemed to notice me. But recently he started looking at me with new eyes, as though he'd never seen me before.'

'I'm very glad for you both,' said Joss with complete truth. 'Now I really must get back to work.' And against Sarah's advice she got carefully to her feet, splashed cold water on her ashen face, applied lipstick with an unsteady hand, then smiled valiantly. 'Right. I'm ready.'

'You look ghastly, Joss,' said Sarah with concern.

'People keep telling me that lately. Very bad for my ego.'

After assuring the various members of staff that she was fully recovered, Joss went outside with Sarah, to find Dan still waiting with Francis.

'How do you feel?' asked Francis anxiously. 'I've got a taxi waiting. We'll get you home right away.'

'I can't do that,' protested Joss. 'I'm due back at work.'

'Don't be an idiot, Joss,' said Dan tersely. 'You look like a ghost. You're obviously coming down with something.'

Secretly Joss felt quite terrible, and in the face of three opposing arguments ran out of strength to argue. 'Oh, very well,' she said wearily, and let Francis hand her into the cab.

'Sarah, move Joss to the middle,' instructed Dan. 'We'd better sit either side of her, in case she keels over again.'

Joss made no attempt to join in the conversation on the journey back to Acton. She felt muzzy, and oddly detached, and the voices of the others came and went in a very confusing way. When the car stopped Sarah and Francis jumped out, but Dan told the driver to wait for a moment before taking them on to Waterloo.

He took Joss by the arm, and looked at Francis. 'I'll see her inside.'

Francis put a restraining hand on Sarah's arm. 'All right, Dan. Ring me later.'

Dan nodded briefly, and asked Joss for her key. He unlocked the door, said goodbye to the others, picked Joss up and carried her inside, kicking the door shut behind him. And Joss, by this time almost totally unaware of what was going on, only registered where she was when her head met the cool comfort of her own pillow. She subsided gratefully, then shot upright, holding her head.

'Must ring Jack Ormond,' she muttered, but Dan pushed her back against the pillows, his large hands surprisingly gentle.

'I'll ring him,' he said firmly. 'Stay where you are.'

Convinced by this time that she was coming down with flu at the very least, Joss did as he said, feeling so ill she had no attention to spare for the fact that Dan was actually here in the flat, where she'd longed for him so much.

'What did Jack say?' she asked, when he came back.

'"If you're infectious stay home until you're not,"' he quoted tersely, and frowned down at her. 'I should have let Sarah stay.'

'Did she want to?'

'Yes. But Francis took her off.'

'Maybe he didn't want her to catch whatever I've got.' She turned her head into the pillow. 'The same applies to you. You'd better go.'

'Do you want me to go?'

In a more normal state of health Joss would have been ecstatic if he'd stayed. But she had a growing conviction that any minute now she was going to lose her lunch. 'Yes, I do. Right now,' she added with sudden urgency.

Dan's face went rigid. He turned on his heel, then paused in the doorway. 'Isn't there someone I could ring to come and take care of you?'

'I'll ring Anna later,' said Joss, swallowing hard. She began to breathe rapidly. 'Go away. *Please.*'

Dan went precipitately, after giving her a look which acted like a green light on her digestive system. He was barely out of the flat before Joss bolted to the bathroom and surrendered to the sickness, which went on for so long she was shaking and cold by the time it was over. With trembling hands she washed her face, then undressed, pulled on a nightshirt and forced herself to go to the kitchen for a bottle of mineral water and a glass. At last she crawled under the covers and surrendered unconditionally to whatever bug was making her feel so ill.

It was dark when Joss woke. She rolled over to look at the clock and found it was after two in the morning. Wonderful, she thought morosely. Now she had a whole night to get through. But to her surprise she found she was hungry. The first thing on the agenda was food. After a visit to the bathroom she went to the kitchen, made tea and toast, curled up on the sofa with the tray beside her, and settled down to watch late-night television until it was time to get up. She stared at the screen with brooding eyes. Now she was feeling better she could have kicked herself for wasting the opportunity to talk to Dan. Not that the occasion had been tailor-made for discussion. After making a spectacle of herself at a very expensive restaurant she couldn't have borne throwing up in front of Dan as an encore.

And now, thought Joss despairingly, she'd told him to go away. So things were back to square one again. She sighed heavily, wriggled deeper into the cushions and tried to think of some other way to see Dan. Maybe she could ask Francis…

When Joss surfaced again she found it was her usual time to get up. And once she'd confirmed, surprised, that she felt normal, she decided she might as well go to work. After a quick shower, she put on her customary white T-shirt and trouser suit, navy linen now in deference to summer, and decided her stomach bug had been one of the lightning, twenty-four-hour variety.

'Joss?' said the news editor, when she reported in. 'I thought you were at death's door.'

'I was for a while,' she said, pulling a face. 'But I'm fine now. What's on for today?'

He gave her a wolfish look. 'The man who rang in to say you were ill yesterday insisted on speaking to me personally. Said his name was Armstrong. Is he, by any strange, wonderful chance, the Armstrong behind Athena?'

Her heart sank. 'Yes,' she admitted unwillingly.

Jack smiled. 'Rumour has it you're involved with him.'

She shook her head. 'Not any more.'

'But you know him well?'

Joss had doubts about that. 'I know him, yes.'

'Dammit, Joss, if he was in your flat when you were ill yesterday you must know him *fairly* well.'

'What's this about, Jack?' she demanded.

'There's a row raging between conservationists and developers over buildings along the Thames. Dan Armstrong is in the front line with the latest Athena development. For once he might welcome the chance to air his point of view. Contact him.'

'No way!' Joss shuddered at the thought of it. 'He doesn't like reporters. Never gives interviews—'

'Precisely!' Jack's eyes fixed on Joss without mercy. 'This could be very good for you careerwise.'

Joss stared him out for a moment, then heaved a sigh. 'Oh, all right. I'll try. But I'm warning you, Jack, I'm not the best person for the job. My relationship with him is over.'

'Oh, yeah?' Jack gave her another of his unsettling smiles. 'He sounded hellish worried when he rang yesterday.'

'Probably afraid of catching my bug!'

With a view to grasping the nettle, Joss dialled the Athena offices the moment she got back to her desk, expecting Dan's assistant to give her the same message as before. But this time, to her astonishment, Joss was put straight through to the man himself.

'Joss? Are you worse?' Dan demanded.

'No, I'm better today. This isn't a personal call.' She breathed in deeply. 'Look, Dan, don't slam the phone down. This isn't my idea—'

'What are you talking about?'

'Jack Ormond wants me to interview you. I told him it was out of the question,' she went on quickly, almost gabbling in her rush to get the conversation over. 'He assumed, because you rang yesterday when I was ill, that we were still—'

'Lovers?' said Dan abrasively.

'Friends,' she corrected. 'I told him we weren't, but he insisted I contact you about your row with the conservationists, to see if you'd like the opportunity to air your views.'

'All right.'

'I'm sorry?' said Joss blankly.

'I said, yes. You can have your interview. When do you want it?'

Joss pulled herself together and told him journalists always want stories yesterday.

'You can have half an hour at seven-thirty tonight.'

'Thank you,' she said faintly.

'Come to the front entrance and tell Security you're expected.'

'Right.' Feeling dazed, Joss went to report her success to the news editor.

On the strength of the coming confrontation with Dan, Joss wheedled her hairdresser into fitting her in at lunchtime on a busy Friday instead of her usual monthly slot, and on the way back afterwards bought a silk camisole to replace her T-shirt, and a pair of very expensive navy linen shoes with four-inch heels as an extra boost. Joss had conducted interviews with every kind of celebrity that caught the public fancy, but this particular interview, she well knew, would be more important and emotionally difficult than all the others rolled into one.

When she arrived at the Athena building just before seven-thirty Joss found it was smaller than she'd expected, and, though modern, blended so well with its surroundings it was a good advertisement for the skill and success of its owner. Squaring her shoulder, Joss pushed open the glass doors, her new heels clicking satisfactorily on the marble floor as she crossed to the desk. She gave her name, and with a pleasant smile the security man escorted her to the lift and pressed the button for the top floor.

'Mr Armstrong is in the office at the end,' he informed her.

When the lift stopped Joss girded herself mentally for battle, then walked along a corridor lined with deserted offices. She knocked on the closed door at the end, took in a deep breath, then in response to Dan's command opened the door and walked in.

CHAPTER EIGHT

THE office was vast, with a panoramic view of the Thames on both sides. Daniel Armstrong rose from behind a large, cluttered desk as she went in, and drew himself up to his full, intimidating height. But courtesy of the new shoes Joss was only a few inches shorter, and stood as erect as he, her eyes unwavering as he motioned her to the chair in front of the desk. Joss sat down with composure, taking mental notes as she looked at the room. The walls were entirely of glass, with the view for sole ornament. The desk was modern and functional, as was the leather sofa along one side of the room, and the entire office was in such stark contrast to the conventional comfort of the house in Kew it was hard to believe the same man inhabited both environments. Dan was wearing a dark city suit with a plain white shirt and rather flamboyant tie, as usual, but fatigue smudged the slanted eyes fixed on her face.

'How are you feeling?' he asked as he resumed his seat. 'I'm surprised you were able to work today. You looked like death when I left yesterday afternoon.'

'I felt it,' Joss agreed. 'But I woke up this morning feeling so much better it seemed pointless to stay at home.'

'Nothing comes between you and the job, of course. I hope this Jack Ormond appreciates your enthusiasm,' he said without inflection, and leaned back in his seat.

'I doubt it,' she said bitterly, and looked at him in appeal. 'I didn't want to do this, Dan.'

He smiled mirthlessly. 'I'm sure you didn't.'

'I never thought for a moment you'd agree.' She met his eyes. 'Why did you?'

He shrugged. 'I might have refused, as usual, if we hadn't met again yesterday.'

'Which doesn't answer my question.'

His eyes hardened. 'There's something I need to know.'

Joss sat very still. 'What is it?'

Dan's mouth tightened. 'Why the hell did you ask me to come round so urgently that night?'

She stared at him blankly. 'I didn't. It was Thursday. I wasn't expecting you.'

'Think back,' he said harshly. 'I was out of the office until late that day. I got back to an urgent message saying that Miss Hunter needed to see me immediately.'

'I didn't leave the message, Dan,' she said flatly. 'Whoever took it got it wrong.'

He raised an eyebrow. 'You expect me to believe that?'

'Yes. I do.' Joss lifted her chin. 'You always approved of my honesty, Dan. Besides, why should I lie?'

'It's a question I've asked myself a hundred times.' Dan's mouth twisted. 'In the circumstances I was surely the last person you wanted to walk in on you—'

'Actually, you're wrong about that.'

He raised a disbelieving eyebrow. 'You surprise me. Unless you wanted an audience for your reunion with the former lover. I assume that's who it was?'

'It was Peter, yes. He rang the bell, I thought it was you, and—'

'Spare me the rest,' he shot at her. 'I saw what happened for myself, heard the little choking noises you were making, heard you saying "please" over and over again as he made love to you—'

'Peter wasn't making *love* to me,' said Joss, incensed. 'He was assaulting me. Couldn't you tell that we were fighting? I was begging him to stop. What you saw was punishment on his part.'

'It didn't look like it,' he threw back at her. 'Not that it matters. If you'd told me about it later it's just possible I might have been able to forget. But because I saw for myself—' He shrugged, his mouth twisting bitterly. 'I just can't blot the scene from my mind.'

The last little flicker of hope died inside Joss. 'So why did you agree to an interview?' she asked quietly.

Dan stared down at the pen he was rolling between his fingers. 'It's a gesture on my part. To give you the interview all the other journalists hound me for.' He looked up. 'I can't blot *you* from my memory, either, Joss. So because of what we had together I decided to give you the exclusive your editor wants.'

The silence lengthened until tension stretched between them to breaking point.

'Payment for services rendered,' Joss said dully. 'An interview instead of a roll of notes left on the dressing table.'

Dan flinched as though she'd struck him, and Joss flung up a hand to silence his reply. 'My gut reaction is to storm out of here and tell you to stuff your interview, Mr Armstrong. But I can't afford the luxury. There are lots of talented people out there after my kind of job. So let's get on with it, shall we?' She put her tape recorder on the desk, pressed the button and smiled encouragingly. 'Tell me, Mr Armstrong, how will conservationist opposition affect the plans for your riverside development?'

Half an hour later Joss pressed the 'stop' button and

put the recorder in her handbag, then got up. 'Thank you very much for seeing me.'

He came round the desk towards her. 'Did you get everything you wanted?'

I want a whole lot more than a stupid interview, raged Joss inwardly. 'Oh, yes,' she said politely. 'More than I'd hoped, in fact.'

The sudden, molten look in Dan's eyes sent her backing away hurriedly.

'I'm glad you got what you wanted,' he growled, advancing on her. 'I wish I could say the same.'

'Keep your distance,' she snapped, eyes flashing. 'You can't say I disgust you one minute, then fancy a spot of fun and games the next.'

His light in his eyes snuffed out abruptly. 'I apologise.'

'For what, exactly?'

'For everything that's happened since we met!' he said in sudden rage. 'Starting with my crass stupidity in following you out on that balcony.'

Joss turned blindly and opened the door, stumbling a little in the new shoes in her hurry to get away, and Dan reached for her and caught her in his arms, his mouth descending towards hers. Then he pushed her away again so violently she stumbled again, and flung a hand out against the wall to right herself.

'It's no good,' Dan said in hoarse anguish. 'I can still see the man's hands on your body, his mouth devouring yours—'

Joss could stand no more. With a choked sound of despair she fled along the corridor to the waiting lift, feeling safe only when she was locked away inside it on her way down to the foyer.

Joss had intended to go to a house-warming one of her friends on Production was hosting, but by the time she

got home it was late, and after the meeting with Dan she
was in no mood for partying. She rang up to plead the
stomach bug as an excuse, then got out her laptop and
typed up the article to release the emotions she'd kept
under control in Dan's office. When she'd polished it she
switched on her mobile phone and transmitted the article
to the *Post*. Afterwards, suddenly remembering she'd
eaten nothing all day, Joss scrambled some eggs, then
after supper had a bath and went to bed to watch television from the comfort of stacked pillows, determined
to get a good night's sleep, for once, in preparation for
her Saturday stint on the *Sunday Globe*.

It was well after midnight when Joss got home the following evening, utterly exhausted. She was so tired she
fell into bed the moment she'd brushed her teeth, and it
was next morning before she bothered to see if there were
any messages. When she heard Dan's voice on the machine her stomach gave a great heave, and before she
could listen to what he had to say she was forced to make
a run for the bathroom. Return of the killer stomach bug,
she thought wretchedly, and washed her sweating face
swiftly so she could get back to the phone.

'Joss, it's Dan,' said the message. 'You looked so pale
last night I was concerned. But if you're out presumably
you're better.'

No, I'm not better, she thought, enraged. Nor was I
out on the town. I was working like a slave to pay for
haircuts and expensive shoes to impress a man who can't
forgive me for something which wasn't my fault. But
that's it. No more. As you once said so emphatically,
Daniel Armstrong, it's finished.

Pride and hard work were poor bedfellows as the summer wore on, with an August so hot Joss found sleeping even more difficult than usual. The article about Dan had been well received by Jack Ormond, and as a result Joss was given more assignments than usual in the time leading up to the week she was taking off to stay at Glebe House for Anna's wedding. She was grateful for the work, which helped a little in her effort to forget the interview with Dan. But when she was alone at night his parting words still burned in her mind like acid. So much so that Joss made no response to his message, and refused to pick up the phone when he rang again to congratulate her on the article. She stood rigid, hands clenched at her side as she listened to Dan's voice thanking her for an accurate and informative piece of writing. He paused, as though he knew she was listening, but with superhuman effort she kept from snatching up the receiver to answer him. The vivid memory of her own fruitless, pleading messages steeled Joss in her resolve.

As the sweltering August dragged by she was eventually forced to face up to a truth so shattering it almost changed her mind about contacting Dan. But only fleetingly. And by then it was time for Anna's wedding. Burying her panic deep, Joss locked up the flat and fled the city to drive off to leafy Warwickshire, and the sanctuary of Glebe House.

'Your friend Francis went to Hugh's stag party,' said Anna, as they lazed in ancient deck chairs in the garden after dinner.

'Really?' Joss chuckled. 'Did Hugh get home in one piece?'

'Yes. Hungover, I gather, but with nothing broken or missing. I laid down the law beforehand. I insist on a bridegroom in mint condition.' She pushed back her mass of curls and eyed Joss closely. 'Heard from Dan since?'

'Yes.'

'And?'

'I didn't pick up the phone.'

'But you still care.'

'Oh, yes,' said Joss wearily. 'I still care.'

'Will you spit and scratch if I say you look fragile, Joss?'

'No. I know very well I look like a hag. It's too hot to sleep in London.' Joss smiled reassuringly. 'But I'll be fine by tomorrow, I promise. Is Francis coming to the wedding, by the way?'

'Yes. And bringing his new fiancée. The eligible Baron's engagement must have saddened the hearts of Dorset debs. What's Sarah like?'

It was restful to chat comfortably in a place which held only memories of childhood. And later, in the familiar narrow bed the Herricks always kept ready for Joss, for the first time in weeks she slept well, and woke so late she found Anna smiling down at her, ready to share the breakfast she'd brought up on a tray.

'Hey!' said Joss, struggling to sit up. She pushed the hair from her eyes and looked at her watch in astonishment. 'It can't be ten!'

'Certainly is. I took Goodfellow out for a ride, then asked Mother for breakfast for two. She was all for cooking eggs, bacon, and everything else in the fridge, but I whittled her down to tea, toast and her celebrated marmalade. OK?'

'Perfect.'' Joss grinned at her windblown friend. 'But it's brides who get breakfast in bed, not guests.'

'You can cart the tray up on the big day, then.'

The week rushed by in wedding preparations, with little time for introspection. But at the rehearsal it was a bittersweet experience for Joss to stand in the church where her father had delivered so many witty sermons. And afterwards, over dinner with the bridegroom and his parents, just to watch Hugh with Anna gave Joss's heart a painful wrench as she contemplated a future without Dan.

But Anna's wedding was too special an occasion to allow private turbulence to intrude on it. Determined that nothing should mar the day, Joss kept her smile firmly in place, and sat with Francis and Sarah and some of Hugh's farming friends for the wedding breakfast in the flower-filled marquee on the lawn, and later on, when Anna and Hugh left on the first stage of their honeymoon, she joined in with the rest to pelt the bridal car with confetti, then accepted with gratitude when Francis and Sarah insisted she had a snack with them in the village inn.

'We thought you might feel a bit flat at this stage,' said Sarah, when Francis was buying drinks at the bar.

'I do, a bit. It's the end of a chapter for Anna and me.' Joss changed the subject quickly. 'So when's *your* wedding?'

Sarah smiled wryly. 'We haven't even had the engagement party yet! Francis is determined to celebrate it at Eastlegh, but it's difficult finding a suitable date that isn't wanted by some company or other.'

'Which is wonderful,' said Joss warmly, and smiled as Francis set three glasses down on the table. 'I hear business is brisk at Eastlegh.'

'Long may it last!' He sat down close to Sarah with a sigh of satisfaction. 'This was a great idea of yours, Joss. A bed for the night here is a better idea than flogging all the way back to Dorset.' He gave her a searching look. 'How are you? Really?'

'I'm fine.'

'You gave us a fright that day at the restaurant,' said Sarah with feeling.

'I frightened myself,' said Joss wryly.

'And Dan,' added Francis.

She shrugged. 'He got over it.'

'I doubt that. Dan's not a happy man these days.' Francis exchanged a look with Sarah. 'Are we allowed to ask what went wrong?'

Joss smoothed the lapel of her silk jacket, avoiding the keen grey eyes. 'He walked in on me when a surprise visitor was getting over-familiar. Against my will, as it happens, but Dan refuses to believe that.' She shrugged philosophically. 'Let's talk about something else.'

It was still early when Sarah and Francis walked Joss back to Glebe House.

'When we finally set a date for our party, will you come, Joss?' asked Francis.

'Will Dan be there?' she asked bluntly.

'He'll be invited.'

'Then I won't—' Joss breathed in sharply, then clutched at Sarah as the starlit night spun round.

Sarah put an arm round her swiftly. 'Joss, shall Francis carry you up to the house?'

'*No!*' Joss breathed in deeply. 'Please—I'm not ill.'

'I think you're pregnant,' said Sarah baldly, and Francis gave a smothered exclamation, and seized Joss's cold hand in his.

'My God—is this true?'

Joss let out a deep, unsteady breath. 'I'm afraid it is.'

CHAPTER NINE

FRANCIS let out a whistle. 'And Dan doesn't know! Are you going to tell him?'

'No *way*.' Joss shuddered at the thought.

'But you must!' said Sarah urgently.

Joss shook her head. 'Fatherhood, he once told me, is definitely not on his agenda. In any case, Dan would never believe the child was his.'

'Because of the incident you mentioned?' asked Francis gently.

'Not exactly.' Joss shivered. 'I met Dan only a short time after breaking up with someone else. How could I expect him to believe me?'

'I think he has the right to know,' said Francis decisively. 'If Sarah were having my child I'd be furious if she didn't tell me.'

'The situation's different, darling,' Sarah pointed out.

'I still think Dan should know—' Francis halted mid-sentence. 'Forgive me, Joss,' he said in sudden contrition. 'It's none of our business.'

'Nothing to forgive. In a way it's a relief to tell someone.' She sighed. 'I couldn't tell Anna, or her mother, before the wedding.'

'What are you going to do?' asked Francis, sounding worried.

'I carry on with my job as long as possible, then hire a nanny afterwards and get back to work. No maternity leave in my kind of job. Nor am I the first lone parent in the world.' Joss kissed them both suddenly. 'Now go

115

back to the pub—and go to bed. Make the most of your time away from Eastlegh.'

'Percipient lady,' said Francis, chuckling, and gave her a hug. 'Sarah won't even move in to Home Farm with me until we tie the knot.'

'We'll keep in touch,' promised Sarah, kissing Joss. 'Please don't feel you're alone in this.'

They saw Joss to the door of Glebe House, thanked the tired Herricks for inviting them to the wedding, then walked down the drive together, waving as they turned through the gates.

'What a charming pair,' said Mrs Herrick, and turned to her husband with a smile. 'Robert, do you think you could make some tea? Joss and I are going to collapse in a heap and indulge in wedding talk.'

'In which case,' he said with a twinkle, 'I'll provide the tea, then smoke a cigar in the garden while I assess damage to the lawn.'

Mrs Herrick chatted about her pleasure in the happy day, then, once her husband had brought in a tea-tray, she filled two cups, sat back in her chair and smiled at Joss.

'You can undo your jacket and be comfortable now, dear. I assume you bought the suit some time ago. How far along are you?'

Joss stared at her in blank dismay. 'Is it written on my forehead? Sarah Wilcox guessed, too.'

'I can't answer for Sarah, but I'm familiar with the signs. Your bust measurement may be bigger, but your face is far too thin. I've had my suspicions all week, Joss.' She smiled affectionately. 'But of course you couldn't tell Anna.'

'No. Not before the wedding, anyway.' Joss undid her jacket with a sigh of relief. 'Thank goodness for that. I moved the jacket buttons to ease the fit. I thought of buying something else, but I'll have to count the pennies from now on.'

'Is Peter Sadler the father?' said Mrs Herrick bluntly.

'No. It's someone I met the night of Anna's engagement party.'

'Does he know?'

Joss shook her head. 'It's my fault I got pregnant. I'd rather soldier on alone.'

'It's your choice about the baby's father, Joss.' Mrs Herrick eyed her sternly. 'However, when your father was ill I promised him we'd take care of you. And we will.'

Anna's mother meant what she said. She rang Joss regularly, with sensible advice, and other regular phone calls came from Sarah and Francis, and, after her return from the Seychelles, from Anna herself.

After the first shock of discovery Anna agreed with Francis, and left Hugh for a night to tell Joss so in person. Dan, she said trenchantly, had the right to know. But Joss was adamant. The mere thought of telling Dan gave her nightmares.

Eventually it was impossible to keep her condition secret, though workwise it made very little difference. She carried on with her job in much the same way as usual, finding she could cope well enough now she was over the dizzy spells and nausea of the initial stage of the pregnancy. But it was October before Joss received the promised invitation to the party at Eastlegh.

'Thanks for asking me, Sarah, but I can't come,' she said adamantly. 'My condition is pretty obvious now. All I lack is a scarlet A on my front.'

'Anna and Hugh are coming,' said Sarah, ignoring her.

'And if you're worried about meeting Dan he's in the States on that date. Probably on purpose. It's not a good idea to drive,' she warned, 'so come by train and put up for the night at Home Farm.'

'Which is a stone's throw from Dan's father's house! Thank Francis very much for the suggestion, but no way am I coming to your party.'

But in the end Joss gave in, because she was tired of the relentless hectoring she'd received on all sides, not least from Anna.

'Oh, all right, all right, I'll come,' she said impatiently at last. 'But I don't have anything to wear. Where can I buy a silk tent?'

'You're not that big. Anyway, Mother's buying the dress,' said Anna, silencing her. 'And if you think you can refuse my mother, Joscelyn Hunter, you're a better woman than me. She's knitting little white things, too.'

Joss wanted to bang her head on the wall. 'Anna, I just hate all this. I always wanted a baby some day. You know that. But not now—not this way.'

'Of course I know,' said Anna in swift sympathy. 'So stop being so damned independent and let us help. We worry.'

Joss took a train from Waterloo on the day of the party, and gazed through the carriage window in pensive mood. Though wild horses wouldn't have dragged the truth from her, she'd changed her mind about telling Dan. A routine scan at the hospital had shown her a little moving entity on the monitor, and Joss had stared at it in wonder, and received a copy of the ultrasound in a state of shock. From that moment on, no matter how often she'd dismissed the change as pure hormonal imbalance, nothing could alter the truth. She was carrying a real live baby born of her love for Daniel Armstrong. Because however hard she tried she couldn't stop loving him, and still missed him so badly that, unknown to her nagging mentors she'd picked up the phone several times to give him the unwanted news. But her courage had always deserted her at the crucial moment.

Francis met her at the station in a battered old Range Rover, and kissed her on both cheeks before lifting her up into the passenger seat. 'You look blooming, Joss.'

'Burgeoning, you mean,' she said dryly. 'You know I didn't want to come.'

'I could hardly fail to! But Sarah's a determined lady.' He chuckled. 'As you probably guessed, she'd decided to marry me long before it dawned on me that she was the perfect wife.'

'I knew that the day you gave me lunch at Home Farm.'

'Talking of which, have you changed your mind about telling Dan?'

Joss shook her head, unable to admit that she had.

Francis changed the subject tactfully, telling her that the Wakefields were waiting for her at Home Farm. 'They wanted to fetch you, but I had to go into Dorchester. Besides,' he added, 'I wanted a word in private before the party.'

When they drove past the brightly lit splendour of Eastlegh Hall to Home Farm, Anna and Hugh came hurrying out to the car, and Francis excused himself to rush off to his room.

'You two show Joss where she's to sleep. I must be ready and waiting with Sarah in the glad rags when the first guests arrive. Anna will give you some tea, Joss, then Hugh will drive you over to the Hall.'

'I can walk that far,' protested Joss.

'Not tonight,' said Hugh firmly. 'You get off, Francis; we'll see to the little mother here.'

'Hugh, for heaven's sake,' Anna remonstrated, but Joss laughed.

'I don't mind. I prefer people to talk about it naturally—makes me feel less like the whore of Babylon.'

'Who the devil was she?' said Hugh, laughing. 'Come on, wife. Give Joss some tea and buns, then bundle her into her party dress at top speed.'

'Bundle being the word,' said Joss ruefully.

Half an hour later she gave a last flick of mascara to her lashes, brushed more colour onto her bottom lip, then eyed herself with reasonable satisfaction in the mirror in one of the Home Farm guest rooms. Now that expensive haircuts were deleted from her budget her hair hung to the shoulders of her dress. She eyed herself wryly. The long, filmy sleeves, and deep, pearl-embroidered neckline could have belonged to any formal dress, but the generous folds of midnight-blue chiffon couldn't quite conceal the bulge where her once-trim waist had been. Joss patted it tenderly, hung pearl drops from her ears, and slid her feet into the navy linen shoes bought to impress Dan at the interview. Four-inch heels were frowned on for mothers-to-be, she thought guiltily, so she would just have to sit down as much as possible. But just for tonight she wanted to show that, far from being embarrassed by it, she was proud of approaching motherhood.

Once she was enveloped in the laughter and music inside Eastlegh Hall Joss enjoyed the party far more than she'd expected. With Hugh and Anna never far away, she circulated among the other guests very happily after the first welcoming hugs and kisses from Sarah and Francis, and after talking to some of the latter's neighbours for a while renewed her acquaintance with

Elizabeth Wilcox, who was full of praise for the article Joss had written on Eastlegh's corporate entertainment venture and called her husband over to add his own appreciation.

The party was a success from the word go, but by the time she'd eaten a delicious supper Joss was feeling the effects of unaccustomed socialising, and her feet were beginning to ache badly in the ridiculous heels. After telling Anna where she was going, Joss slipped out onto the terrace for some badly needed fresh air, her eye on one of the ornamental stone benches some former Morville had brought back from Italy after the Grand Tour. With a sigh of relief she sank onto the cold seat and eased off the shoes, thankful that the autumn night was mild enough to sit in comfort for a few minutes.

By the light of the full moon Home Farm and the Armstrong cottage were plainly visible in the distance. Joss sighed. She had disciplined herself to avoid thinking too much about Dan lately, but here, in these surroundings, it was impossible. She knew Dan had won his battle about the riverside development, but otherwise had had no news of him. She stared out into the moonlit night, wondering what Dan was doing in the States. And who he was doing it with. Then Joss heard footsteps on the stone flags, and bent hurriedly to thrust her feet into the crippling shoes. She looked up with a bright smile, prepared to make excuses for her sudden yearning for solitude. Then her eyes widened in shock as she saw a tall, unmistakable figure standing with a glass in each hand. Joss blinked, feeling as though she'd pressed a replay button on a video recorder. Barring one important detail, the scene was almost identical to their first meeting.

'Hello, Joss. I was told you were out here,' said Dan quietly.

Joss pinned the smile firmly back in place. 'Daniel Armstrong, no less. For a moment I thought I was seeing things.'

'Back in the same movie,' he agreed.

'Something like that. Why aren't you in America?'

'Why should I be?'

'Sarah told me you were.'

The sudden silence was all the more marked for the sounds of laughter and conviviality in the background.

'For probably the only time in her life Sarah was telling lies,' said Dan. 'I assume,' he added carefully, 'that if you'd known I was here you wouldn't have come.'

'Probably not,' she said lightly. 'Though I found it hard to believe you'd miss your oldest friend's celebration. Are you pleased that he's marrying Sarah?'

'Of course I am. I've been expecting it for years.'

Joss smiled. 'Francis must have been the last one to realise they were made for each other.'

Dan shrugged. 'Not everyone falls in love at first sight.'

'No,' said Joss, her face suddenly shadowed. 'Outside of fiction very few, probably.' She braced herself, nerving herself up for confrontation. Showtime. No point in dragging it out. 'Is one of those glasses for me?' she asked, and moved forward into the light to take one.

Dan took an incredulous look and dropped one of the glasses on the stone flags.

'Joss?' cried Anna, rushing out with Hugh. 'I heard a crash. Are you all right?'

'Yes. I'm fine. You remember Dan Armstrong, of course?' said Joss with composure.

The three of them muttered automatic greetings, but when Joss moved closer Dan shoved the glass in his hand at Hugh and leapt forward, hands outstretched to keep her back. 'Don't move; there's glass everywhere.'

'I'll get someone,' said Hugh, and whisked a reluctant Anna away, leaving a deafening silence behind them.

'What's known as a pregnant pause,' said Joss at last, deliberately flippant.

'How can you treat it so lightly?' he demanded bitterly, then broke off with a curse as two of Elizabeth Wilcox's team hurried outside to clear up the broken glass. He seized Joss by the hand. 'It's hot inside—fancy a walk in the moonlight?' he said urgently, winning indulgent smiles from the women who'd known him all his life.

'Lovely,' lied Joss, and let him lead her down the steps, doing her best to ignore the crippling shoes.

'Why are you limping?' he demanded as they reached the gravelled terrace below.

'My feet hurt.'

'I suppose you're tottering on six-inch heels as usual,' he said irritably.

'Four-inch tonight.'

'Rather stupid in your condition.'

'My condition is my own concern,' she snapped, wincing as his grasp threatened to cut off her circulation.

'Surely it's also the concern of the man involved!'

'Not in this case.'

'You haven't told him?'

'No.'

'Why the hell not?'

Joss spotted a bench at the edge of the knot garden. 'Can we sit, please? Otherwise I may never walk again.'

Dan made for the bench in silence, then sat beside her, studying her face in the moonlight. 'Is Sadler the father?' he asked at last.

'Certainly not,' said Joss, eyeing his clenched fists.

'Then is it mine, for God's sake?' he demanded, as though the words were torn from him.

'Of course it is,' said Joss, and turned her head to look at him.

'Is this the truth?' he asked hoarsely.

'Yes. And nothing but the truth, so help me God. Whether you believe it or not is up to you, of course.' Joss smiled comfortingly. 'But don't worry, Dan. Even if you do believe me I'm not asking you to do anything about it.'

'Don't be so stupid,' he roared at her.

'For heaven's sake,' she said irritably. 'You'll have Hugh charging to the rescue if you bellow like that.'

Dan controlled himself with obvious effort. 'Is this the reason for your phone calls after—'

'After you found me in what you took to be *flagrante* with Peter Sadler,' she said with composure. 'As a matter of fact, no. I didn't know then.'

'When did you find out?'

'My embarrassing faint at the restaurant that day was the start of it. I kept feeling so weird from time to time after that I eventually saw a doctor.'

'Surely you had an idea what was wrong!'

'No. The usual indications were conspicuous by their presence, not their absence. It happens sometimes, apparently.' Joss shrugged philosophically. 'And I mistook my lack of appetite and so on for something else entirely.'

'What do you mean?'

She laughed scornfully. 'Use your imagination, Daniel Armstrong. I was in seventh heaven about to set up house with you, then *wham*. You dumped me, wouldn't answer my calls, refused to have anything to do with me. Your attitude was a pretty effective appetite depressant.'

'I did call you, after the interview. More than once.' He looked down into her face. 'Were you always out when I rang?'

'No. I heard you every time.'

'And refused to pick up the phone.' His mouth twisted. 'Was revenge sweet?'

'Yes,' Joss said frankly. 'It was.' She got to her feet, wincing. 'Time we returned to the festivities.'

Dan leapt up, and seized her hands. 'We can't leave things like this. When's the child due?'

'In early spring.'

Dan held her hands wide, staring down at the curve filling out her dress. 'That first night, you told me there was no danger of this.'

She detached her hands, and began to walk. 'I'd forgotten that I gave up on birth-control after Peter walked out. I only started again after your reappearance in my life. Not quite soon enough, unfortunately.'

'Unfortunate indeed,' he agreed, pacing beside her. 'I remember your views on motherhood only too well.'

'Yours on fatherhood were even more negative,' she said tartly. 'Is it any wonder I didn't tell you I was pregnant?'

'I had a right to know.'

'So everyone keeps telling me.'

Dan halted in his tracks, holding her by the shoulders. 'So everyone knows I'm your child's father except me?'

'Only the people who matter.'

'And I don't!' he said bitterly.

Joss removed his hands. 'Last time we met you said you couldn't bear to touch me. How on earth did you expect me to tell you I was carrying your child?'

'If you'd answered my calls you'd know I'd got over that,' he said gruffly, as they resumed walking.

'You knew where I lived, Dan,' she pointed out.

'I've driven round more than once,' he said savagely, astonishing her. 'I was parked along your street one night, waiting, when you arrived home with two other women. The next time you never arrived at all. I found out later from Francis that you were in Warwickshire with Anna. Then I went to the States. When I came back Francis said you were coming to the party, so I thought I'd wait, bide my time until you felt less bitter towards me. But I was held up at Athena and arrived late tonight, at which point Francis told me you were out on the terrace. So I decided to try a rerun of our first meeting.'

'And got the shock of your life!'

He nodded grimly. 'Why the hell didn't Francis warn me?'

'He feels—quite rightly—that it isn't his business.' Joss caught sight of Anna and Hugh coming towards them. 'Time to join the party again. Francis must be about to make the formal announcement. After which,' she added, wincing as she stumbled, 'I'm going back to Home Farm to bed. I'm tired.'

Dan held her arm in an iron grip. 'How did you travel down? I hope you didn't drive yourself in your con—'

'If you mention the word "condition" I'll scream,' she informed him. 'I came by train.'

'Then I'll drive you back,' he said promptly.

'No, thanks. I prefer the train.'

Secretly Joss felt rather crestfallen when Dan said no more, and because Hugh and Anna came hurrying to herd them back to the Hall for the big moment she had no more private conversation with him until she'd kissed Sarah and Francis goodnight, and it was time to leave for Home Farm.

'I'll see you tomorrow,' Dan stated, after Hugh had gone to fetch the car.

With Anna's eyes on them Joss couldn't bring herself to object. 'Goodnight, then,' she said politely.

Dan took his leave of them both with punctilious courtesy, and handed Joss into Hugh's car as though she were a time bomb about to explode, something Anna commented on with great satisfaction once the car moved off.

'How did he react?' she demanded.

'Stunned disbelief. You saw the smashed glass,' said Joss, yawning. 'Gosh, I'm tired.'

'You'd better let us drive you home tomorrow,' said Anna. 'A train journey on top of tonight is a very bad idea.'

'Certainly not; it's miles out of your way,' said Joss firmly. 'I like travelling by train.'

Rather to her surprise Joss slept very well that night, and woke only when Anna came rushing in to announce that Dan was downstairs, demanding her presence.

'At this hour? Demanding?' said Joss, scowling as she struggled to sit up.

'More or less. Imperious bloke, isn't he?'

'He'll just have to wait.' Joss swung her feet to the floor, then breathed in sharply, biting her lip.

'What's the matter?' asked Anna in alarm.

Joss pointed to two hugely swollen ankles and feet, and sighed despairingly. 'The price of vanity.'

'I *told* you not to wear those shoes!'

'But I did. And now I can't wear any shoes at all.' Joss stood up with difficulty, muttering something rude under her breath. 'Now what do I do!'

'Have a bath. Maybe the swelling will go down.'

'Good idea. Tell Dan he's in for a long wait.'

But neither a bath, nor the quantities of cold water Joss

poured over them afterwards, did anything to reduce the size of her feet. In the end she gave up, pulled on black jersey trousers with a drawstring waist, and a large Cambridge-blue sweater bought in the men's department of her favourite chainstore, then brushed her hair swiftly as a peremptory hand beat a tattoo on the door.

'Joss?' called Dan. 'Are you all right?'

Joss hobbled painfully across the room and opened the door. Dan stood outside on the landing, looking so good in faded old jeans and an indigo shirt she felt a leap of unwanted response.

'Good morning,' he said, eyeing her feet.

'If you say a word about silly shoes I'll punch you in the nose,' said Joss fiercely.

He looked up, smiling crookedly. 'You and whose army, Joscelyn Hunter?'

She tucked a strand of hair behind her ear, glaring at him.

'I came to deliver an invitation,' he said, surprising her.

'Invitation?'

'From my father. He liked the piece you did about Eastlegh. Asked if you'd have coffee with him this morning.'

Joss stared at him in surprise, then gestured at her front. 'Does he know about this?'

'No.'

Joss shook her head vigorously. 'Then please explain that I can't come due to my feet.'

'I brought the car. I can carry you downstairs and drive you over,' said Dan, and eyed the swollen feet, frowning. 'Do you have any socks?'

'Yes. But they won't go on. And I refuse to go anywhere barefoot *and* pregnant,' she snapped, her colour rising.

Anna came hurrying up the stairs, with Hugh behind her. 'How are the feet?'

'Large as life, unfortunately.'

Dan shot a glance at Hugh. 'Could you lend her a pair of socks?'

'Of course.' Hugh grinned. 'What colour do you fancy, Joss?'

'Size is the priority, not colour, Hugh Wakefield,' she said tartly, red to the roots of her hair as the other three gazed at the offending extremities. 'Could everyone stop that, please?'

Anna took her arm. 'Sit down while *I* choose the socks. Afterwards you can carry her downstairs, Dan.'

'There's no need for that,' said Joss explosively, then proved herself wrong when her progress to the nearest chair resembled a walk over hot coals.

'How do you feel? Other than the feet,' asked Dan, when they were alone.

Joss glared at him. 'Just dandy.'

'No more fainting?'

'No.'

His eyes dropped to the bulge. 'Is the baby fine too?'

'Yes. I've got a snapshot to prove it. An ultrasound photograph,' she added hurriedly at the look on his face. 'If you'll hand me that bag over there I'll show you.'

When Joss handed the copy over Dan studied it in awe. 'Do you know what sex it is?'

Joss shook her head. 'No. I preferred to wait.'

Anna came hurrying in, brandishing a pair of large black socks. 'Thank goodness Hugh has enormous feet. Try these.' She knelt in front of Joss and drew the socks gently over the swollen feet. Joss nodded.

'Fine.'

Dan bent and picked her up. 'I'll carry you down to the car.'

'Car?' said Anna. 'She's not leaving until after lunch.'

'I'm taking her to have coffee with my father,' said Dan rather breathlessly, descending the stairs with care. 'It's all right,' he told Anna over Joss's head when they reached the hall. 'I'll look after her.'

'Don't keep her long. She hasn't had any breakfast,' said Anna anxiously, as she went with them to the door.

'When did I ever eat breakfast!' said Joss.

'Then it's time you started,' grunted Dan in disapproval. 'Don't worry, Anna. I'll see she gets something to eat.'

'I don't want this,' said Joss mutinously, once they were on the way to his father's cottage.

'No. I don't suppose you do. But my father obviously took a fancy to you. Not,' added Dan, 'something he does very often.'

Joss sighed despondently. 'He'll probably change his mind when he sees I'm pregnant.'

Dan gave a bark of mirthless laughter. 'Why the hell should he do that?'

She flushed irritably. 'Does he know any single mothers?'

'Francis employs two of them. My father's unlikely to go into shock at the sight of you.'

Sam Armstrong came out of the house as the car stopped. His weathered face wore a welcoming look as he opened the car door. 'Come in, Miss Hunter.' He offered her his hand, and Joss took it, her heart in her throat as the keen old eyes took in the unmistakable bulge.

'Father, I'll have to carry Joss into the house,' Dan warned. 'She can't get any shoes on.'

Sam Armstrong stood back, his face unreadable as he watched his son scoop Joss from her seat.

'Best bring her in front of the fire, Dan,' he said without comment. 'It's a bit nippy this morning.'

Dan deposited Joss in one of the leather armchairs drawn up to the fire in the familiar sitting room. 'I'll make the coffee,' he said swiftly. 'Joss hasn't had any breakfast.'

'Slice some bread, then,' said Sam, seating himself in the other chair. 'Bring it in and I'll toast it in front of the fire.' He reached under his chair, pulled out a footstool and pushed it near Joss. 'Put your feet on that, my dear.'

'Thank you. It's lovely. Was it your wife's?' asked Joss, admiring the stool's finely worked tapestry cover.

'Yes—she was clever with a needle.' Sam grimaced. 'Now it's mine. I get the odd bit of gout.'

'And doesn't take his pills,' said Dan, bringing in a platter of bread. 'I'll bring butter with the coffee.'

Now the initial ordeal was over Joss felt oddly comfortable alone with Sam Armstrong, watching with pleasure as he held slices of bread over the flames with a copper toasting fork. 'I haven't had proper toast since I left home,' she remarked.

Sam turned to look at her. 'Dan says your father was a vicar.'

Joss nodded. 'I miss him a lot. Especially now,' she added, patting her front.

'I hear you were seeing a lot of Dan, then there was some kind of quarrel,' said Sam, going on with his task.

'Yes.'

'Is my son the father of your child?' asked Sam bluntly, taking Joss's breath away.

'Yes, I am,' said Dan, dumping a coffee tray on the

table. He shot a look at Joss. 'Are you all right? Your colour went for a moment.'

'My house guest just did a little dance,' she said breathlessly.

Dan filled a coffee cup and handed it to her, then hunkered down in front of the fire to butter two slices of bread. He handed her the plate, then looked at his father. 'No comment?' he demanded.

Sam Armstrong gave his son a piercing look. 'Joscelyn tells me her father's dead. So I'll speak for him. In my day it was simple. If a girl got pregnant the baby's father married her.'

'Which is precisely what I'm going to do—now I've finally been informed,' said Dan with emphasis, and returned his father's look. 'And not because *you* think I should, either. I decided that the moment I discovered Joss was pregnant.'

'And when was that?' demanded Sam.

'Last night,' said Joss, deciding to put her oar in. 'But you must realise that the decision isn't up to Dan, Mr Armstrong. It's up to me. And I don't want to get married.'

The disapproval in the two pairs of identical blue eyes was almost amusing. Joss smiled gently. 'I prefer to manage on my own.'

Dan got to his feet, looming over her with such menace Joss exerted considerable self-control not to cower in her chair. 'Don't be silly,' he said coldly. 'We'll get married as soon as I can arrange it.'

'We will not!' Her eyes flashed dangerously. 'Not so long ago you couldn't bear the sight of me.'

'That's not true,' he said, his voice dangerously quiet. 'And this is no place to discuss it. But get this straight. When I decide I want something, I get it.'

Sam stared at his son in disbelief. 'Are you mad, boy? That's no way to make a proposal of marriage.'

'You keep out of it, Father,' his son shot at him.

'He wasn't proposing, Mr Armstrong,' said Joss scornfully. 'He was acquiring a property. Buying a wife, just as he bought his title.'

Sam stared at her blankly. 'What title?'

'She means the manorial title I bought from Francis,' said Dan impatiently.

Sam wagged a finger at Joss. 'Now you listen, young lady. Young Francis—Lord Morville, I mean—owes a lot to my son.'

'Father!' warned Dan. 'Keep out of this.'

Sam rose to his feet with effort, then straightened to look his son in the eye. 'I'll go in the kitchen and see to the meal. While I'm out talk to the girl like a human being. She's not a board meeting.'

After he'd gone the only sound in the room was the crackling of flames from the fire. Joss went on eating her toast, hungry despite the tension in the air, and determined that if anyone was going to break the silence it would be Dan. He took his father's chair, leaned forward with hands clasped loosely between his knees, gazing into the flames for a while. At last he cleared his throat, turned to look at her, and said, 'Joss, let's start again. Will you—?'

CHAPTER TEN

SUDDENLY the door flew open and Francis came in like a whirlwind, halting Dan mid-sentence. 'Why the devil can't you bend that stiff neck of yours, Dan, and tell Joss the simple truth?'

Dan leapt to his feet, glaring at him. 'And why the devil can't you mind your own business?'

'This *is* my business,' drawled Francis, suddenly very much the ninth Baron Morville. He stared Dan out, then turned to Joss. 'Forgive me. How are you this morning? Anna tells me you find walking difficult.'

'A self-inflicted problem, alas.' Joss managed a smile.

'What are you doing here, anyway?' demanded Dan, looking like thunder.

'Anna told me you'd brought Joss here so I came over to see how she was. On the way in your father told me you were being pig-headed about telling her the truth.'

'Did he, by God?' said Dan, striding to the door.

'Dan,' said Joss sharply. 'Come back here. Stop behaving like a barbarian.'

He turned to stare at her in such blank shock that Francis began to laugh.

'I think you've met your match, old son.' He put out a hand in appeal. 'Look at it from my point of view. I insist Joss knows the facts.'

Dan's face relaxed slightly. 'Then of course I've no choice—milord.'

'Pack it in, Dan,' said Francis irritably. 'And for

heaven's sake sit down. I can't talk with you looming over me.'

When Dan took his father's chair again Francis perched himself on the arm.

'As I told you once before, Joss,' he began, 'like a lot of my kind I'm perpetually short of funds when it comes to the upkeep of Eastlegh. And Dan, in his own way, is just as attached to the place as I am. So he continually thinks up ways for me to acquire money to keep it going.'

Dan, Francis went on, had asked to buy the gardener's tied cottage, plus some land to grow vegetables, thus giving Sam Armstrong a home he could call his own at last, and at the same time providing an infusion of cash for Eastlegh. Then later, when the auctioning of manorial titles gained in popularity, Dan had hit on the idea of buying one of Francis's extraneous titles to add to the deeds of a local manor house his company had restored, again a two-way benefit, as this had doubled the asking price of the finished property.

'But the real brainwave came when Dan asked if he could hire Eastlegh for a weekend conference Athena was hosting,' added Francis.

'Lord Morville, of course,' said Dan dryly, 'was all for letting me have the place for free.'

'But Dan stipulated a business transaction or nothing doing. And thus,' finished Francis with a hint of drama, 'was born the now flourishing Eastlegh corporate entertainment business.'

'Was it your idea for Francis to move into Home Farm, Dan?' asked Joss.

'No, that was mine,' said Francis. 'It was obvious that I'd have more to offer if I could hire out the entire house. I love Eastlegh, but's a big place to rattle round in on my own.' He smiled. 'So now you know, Joss. Dan never had the slightest desire to be lord of anyone's manor.'

Dan gave her a sardonic look. 'My motive, as always, was profit.'

'So, Joss, does all this make you better disposed to marrying Dan?' asked Francis, then winced as a hard hand clamped on his arm like a vice.

'I'd be grateful for just a *few* minutes' privacy to make my own proposals,' said Dan with sarcasm, 'so do me a favour—take my father off to admire his beloved garden, and give me ten minutes alone with Joss.'

'Yes, of course,' said Francis hastily, jumping to his feet. He bent to kiss Joss, grinned at Dan, then went from the room as quickly as he'd arrived.

'It seems I owe you an apology,' said Joss unwillingly.

Dan shrugged. 'Not really.'

'Though you deliberately mentioned the title at lunch that day to mislead me,' she said, eyes kindling.

He snorted. 'I thought you couldn't stay meek and mild for long!'

Joss glared at her swollen feet in frustration, yearning to jump up and follow Francis from the room.

'One way and another,' he said, reading her mind with ease, 'this time you can't perform your famous vanishing trick.'

'No,' she said shortly. 'In which case you can pour me another cup of coffee.'

Dan obliged in silence, then sat down again, a determined look in his eye. 'As I was saying before His Lordship interrupted us, we'd better get married, Joss.'

She gazed at him in silence for so long Dan began to frown. 'No,' she said at last.

He stared at her, incensed. 'What do you mean, no?'

'The opposite of yes.'

'You're enjoying yourself,' he said angrily. 'Look, Joss, I know I hurt you—'

'You certainly did,' she agreed. 'But don't worry, I've got over that now.' Her eyes clashed with his. 'I'm good at getting over things.'

The irritation drained from his face, taking the animation with it. 'In which case,' he went on after a tense pause, 'if I suggested a marriage in form only, for the sake of our child, would you at least agree to that?'

'A marriage of convenience?' said Joss, taking great pleasure in watching Dan's struggle to control his temper. 'How delightfully archaic. Like a Regency romance.'

'You obviously find all this hilarious,' he said harshly. 'I happen to think it's a bloody serious situation.'

'So do I,' she assured him, and shifted a little in her seat. The second cup of coffee had been a mistake. 'I'm afraid,' she said reluctantly, 'I need your assistance.'

'What's the matter?' he demanded, leaping to his feet.

She sighed. 'Unlike heroines in Regency romances, I need to go to the bathroom. I hope your father's got one on the ground floor.'

Dan's lips twitched. 'So do I. You weigh a ton these days.'

'Your proposal technique could do with polish,' she flashed at him, and put her hands flat on the arms of the chair, so obviously prepared to struggle unaided that Dan cursed under his breath.

'Let me help you, Joss. Please.'

She gave him a dark, hostile look, but in the end let him take her hands and carefully pull her upright. Her teeth sank into her bottom lip as her throbbing feet took her weight, and with a look which dared her to object Dan picked her up and carried her along the hall and out into a back entry, where a door led into a very modern little cloakroom.

'Can you manage now?' he said with constraint.

'Yes,' Joss snapped, and shut the door in his face. When she emerged Sam Armstrong was waiting outside with Dan.

'Are you all right, my dear?' he asked, winning a surprised look from his son.

'Yes, thanks,' she said philosophically. Dignity, she was learning, was a luxury abandoned with the onset of pregnancy.

Dan picked her up again, then paused in the hall. 'Where do you want to go now?' he asked.

'Put her back by the fire until our meal is ready,' said Sam with authority.

When they were alone again, Joss watched as Dan added more logs to the fire. 'I'm bidden to lunch, then.'

He shot her a wry look. 'Apparently. My father seems to take it for granted you'll stay. He doesn't entertain much. You're honoured.'

'It's very kind of him,' she said soberly.

There was an awkward silence for a moment, broken only by the clashing of pots and pans from the kitchen. At last Dan broke it to ask about her work, and Joss responded with relief, eager to abandon the topic of marriage.

'I ought to be out there, giving your father a hand,' she added impatiently at one point.

'Which you can't, so stay where you are.'

'I don't have much choice!'

Dan's mouth twisted. 'You don't have a choice in any of this,' he said bitterly. 'I remember your views on motherhood all too vividly—but an apology's just an insult.'

'And unnecessary,' she informed him.

'I disagree.' Dan stared into the fire. 'I should have been more careful. But it's too damn late to say that now.'

'Look, Dan,' Joss began, doing her best to be reasonable. 'I know that a child was never part of your plan—' She broke off, smiling as Sam Armstrong came into the room. 'I wish I could help, Mr Armstrong. Something smells delicious.'

'Just plain cooking,' he said gruffly, looking pleased. 'The same as every Sunday. You'd better lay the small table in here, Dan.'

Two hours later Joss was sitting, resigned, in Dan's car on the way back to London. 'Sorry to add to your journey,' she said eventually, as they left Dorchester.

He shot a sidelong glance at her. 'If you want to apologise it should be for letting me find out about the baby in public.'

'I didn't know you were going to be there.'

'Or you wouldn't have come within miles of Eastlegh,' he finished for her. 'As a matter of interest, when *were* you going to tell me?'

When Joss made no answer, his hands tightened, white-knuckled, on the steering wheel. 'Never?' he demanded harshly.

'What was the point? I was sure you'd refuse to believe the child was yours, especially after you found Peter Sadler in my flat that night.'

'I suppose I can understand that,' he said grudgingly, then fell silent. 'You know Joss,' he said at last, 'I'm still in the dark about certain aspects of that night. I got your message, drove like a bat out of hell to your place, and then found your door ajar. I shot up those stairs, expecting to mug a burglar at the very least.'

'I didn't send any message—but don't let's go over all that again,' she said wearily. 'It's all in the past.'

'But the child is in the future, Joss.'

'I know,' she said quietly, with a familiar tremor of apprehension at the mere thought of it.

'Have you made plans?'

She repeated her idea of hiring a nanny and returning to work as soon as possible after the birth.

'With no time at all to spare for the baby?' he demanded incredulously.

Joss made a superhuman effort to control her temper. 'As you mentioned earlier, I don't have any choice.'

'Of course you do,' he retorted grimly. 'You can stop being so damned pig-headed and marry me.'

'When you make the prospect sound so delightful,' she threw back, 'it's hard to refuse. But I do, just the same.'

'This isn't the time and place to discuss it,' said Dan coldly, as they hit heavier traffic. 'We'll talk again when we get home.'

The journey was a trial, made worse by an embarrassing request for a stop at a service station. Joss flatly refused to let Dan carry her, and after she'd hobbled back to the car with his help she sat in silence, trying to relay pleasant thoughts to the little intruder making its presence felt under her sweater. But when they were nearing London it dawned on her that Dan was taking her to his own home in Kew.

'I want to go straight to my place,' she said, very quietly.

'Not yet,' said Dan inexorably. 'We finish our talk before I drive you to Acton.'

By this time Joss was beginning to feel very weary. 'Oh, very well,' she sighed. 'But there's not really much point.'

When they arrived at the house Dan bent to lift her out of the car, but Joss held him off.

'No, please. I can walk. Well, hobble, really, but I can manage.'

Tight-lipped, he put a hand under her elbow and helped her into the house Joss had believed she'd never set foot in again. Dan released her outside the ground floor cloakroom, eyeing her warily.

'I'll make some tea. Are you hungry?'

Joss shook her head. 'I'm still full of roast lamb and your father's heavenly vegetables. But tea sounds wonderful.'

In the privacy of Dan's cloakroom Joss eyed her reflection without pleasure, tidied herself a little, then with a sigh went outside, to find Dan waiting to escort her into the comfortable, informal room which opened into the courtyard at the back of the house.

Joss sat down in a corner of Dan's vast sofa, and smiled her thanks as he pushed a couple of cushions under her feet.

'Lack of footstools here.' He handed her a beaker of tea. 'No sugar and just a splash of milk,' he said, then shot a look at her. 'Or has your taste changed lately?'

'No,' she assured him. Her taste was exactly the same, both for tea and present company. Suddenly she noticed the initial J in black italic on the tall white porcelain mug she held.

'I bought it when you were about to move in with me,' Dan said without inflection.

Joss bit her lip, suddenly overwhelmed by thoughts of what might have been. She sat drinking her tea, deep in reverie, then gave herself a mental shake and looked round at the comfortable, masculine room as he took a chair opposite her. 'Dan.'

'Yes?' he said swiftly.

'The night we met—'

'I haven't forgotten it,' he said dryly.

'I've just thought of something. In fact,' Joss added, 'I'm surprised I never thought of it before.'

'Go on.'

'You suggested room service at the hotel. Why were you staying there when you had this to come back to?'

To her astonishment, colour rose along his cheekbones.

'I wasn't staying there,' he said gruffly. 'But if you'd said yes I would have reserved a room while you were saying goodnight to Anna.'

Joss stared at him. 'Then you planned to get me to bed right from the first.'

'No,' he said coldly. 'You disliked the idea of a restaurant, and this place is a long way out of town. So I suggested a meal in my non-existent room. The invitation to your place came as a surprise.'

She smiled coolly. 'A convenient one, too. Look at the money I saved you.'

The dark blue eyes locked with hers. 'I would have paid anything the hotel asked, just to keep you with me a while longer.'

Joss stared back, silenced, her heart beating thickly under the sweater.

'You know I wanted you the moment I first saw you,' he went on conversationally, as though they were discussing the weather. Then his eyes lit with sudden heat. 'I still do.'

Wanting, thought Joss fiercely, wasn't enough. 'It's not much of a basis for marriage.'

'We've got a lot more going for us than that,' said Dan swiftly, sensing victory.

Joss looked at him narrowly. 'What do you mean?'

He frowned. 'The child, of course.'

Her little flame of hope flickered and died. 'Ah, yes. The child,' she repeated, as though the idea were new to her. 'Not something you ever wanted.'

'I admit I wasn't enthusiastic about the idea in theory,' he admitted. 'But now it's established fact I'm fully prepared to share the responsibility.'

'Very noble,' she snapped. 'But you don't have to marry me to do that.'

'True. But marriage is a practical option.' Dan put down his tea untouched.

Practical, she thought sadly, and smiled a little. 'You look as though you need something stronger than that.'

'Damn right I do. But I still have to drive you home.'

'There are usually taxis to be had, even in the wilds of Kew!'

He raised a sardonic eyebrow. 'And what happens if you can't make it up the stairs when you get to your place?'

Joss clenched her teeth. Crawling up her stairs on hands and knees was a lot preferable to sitting here listening to Daniel Armstrong talking about responsibility. Especially when one solitary word of love would put an end to all argument.

'I'll manage,' she said tightly.

Dan's eyes narrowed. 'Not if I keep you here until you agree to marry me.'

Her eyes flashed scornfully. 'First Regency, now the Middle Ages. You're no feudal lord, Dan, and I'm not some kidnapped heiress.'

'If you'd wanted a lord for a husband you should have aimed for Francis!'

'I don't want a husband of any kind,' lied Joss. 'I can manage on my own.'

'So I see,' said Dan with sarcasm, then took her breath away by sliding to his knees in front of her. But instead of proposing in true romantic style, as for one wild moment she'd thought he meant to, he pulled off Hugh's socks to examine her still swollen feet. 'And just how do you propose to get to work tomorrow on feet like pillows?'

'The swelling will be down tomorrow,' she croaked, choked with disappointment.

Dan slid the socks carefully back into place, then got to his feet. 'More tea?'

'No, thanks. I want to go home.' Joss put the mug down carefully on the table beside her, passionately wishing she could get to her feet unaided. Without a word Dan reached down his hands to take hers, and equally silent she took them, and allowed him to help her up.

'Stay here tonight, Joss—please,' he said urgently. 'I'll sleep in one of the spare rooms and drive you home in the morning. Once I'm sure you can walk.'

Joss gave up. She was tired, and suddenly so depressed she didn't care where she slept. 'All right,' she said listlessly. 'As long as I can go to bed right now. Will you fetch my things from the car, please?'

He scowled. 'But the whole object of your staying is to talk this through. And you should have something to eat—'

'No,' she said flatly. 'I meant it, Dan. I'm tired. I need bed—and solitude.'

His eyes hardened. 'If you object to my company that much I'll drive you back to Acton right now.'

'Which,' she said, incensed, 'is what I wanted all along.'

Joss would have given much to march out of Daniel Armstrong's house with her nose in the air, but in the end was forced to accept his arm back to the car. And once they were on their way she felt so miserable it took superhuman effort to keep from crying her eyes out. Damned hormones, she thought, sniffing, and glowered at the large hand offering a box of tissues.

'Thank you,' she said with dignity.

'Why are you crying?' asked Dan.

'I don't need a reason these days.' She sniffed loudly. 'I suppose it was a bit ambitious to travel down to Eastlegh and go to the party last night on top of a working week.'

'Why did you?'

'Because Anna felt a bit of socialising would do me good. She kept on and on about it. And Sarah was on the phone so much I wonder she had time to organise the party.'

'Francis was damned insistent where I was concerned, too.' Dan shot a glance at her. 'It was obviously a combined effort to enlighten me about the baby.'

'Probably. I made Francis swear on oath that he wouldn't tell you.'

'Which gagged him pretty effectively.'

'He thought you had a right to know.'

'Would you really have kept me in the dark, Joss? Even after the baby arrived?'

Joss shrugged, her eyes on the traffic in front of them. 'I intended to. I think I'd have kept to that. But fate—and friends—conspired against me.'

By the time they got to Acton Joss was sorry she hadn't stayed the night at Kew after all. She felt desperately tired, vaguely unwell, her feet hurt and she wished she hadn't eaten so much lunch. When Dan came to help her out of the car he took one look at her face and demanded her key.

When Joss meekly handed it over he unlocked the door and picked her up, ignoring her protests as he carried her upstairs to deposit her very carefully on her sofa. 'I'll just get your belongings, then I want no argument, Joss. You look exhausted. Before I go I want to make sure you're in bed and out of harm's way for the night.'

'Will you give me a hand to the bathroom first?' she asked, resigned.

When Dan got back with her suitcase Joss was leaning in the bathroom doorway, her face chalk-white. He leapt towards her, arms outstretched, his face suddenly as colourless as hers.

'What is it?'

'Something's wrong, Dan,' she said hoarsely.

A few hours later Joss lay propped against pillows in a hospital bed in a private room, feeling so tired it was an effort to summon a smile for Dan.

'You look terrible,' she commented, eyeing his haggard face.

'Never mind me!' He sat by the bed to take her hand. 'I had a word with the consultant, and apparently the baby's fine. But they want to keep you in for a couple of days for observation, and after that you're to stay off your feet for a while, and rest.'

'I know,' said Joss despondently. 'She told me.'

'You know what this means?' he said, his grasp tightening.

She nodded glumly. 'Time off from the job.'

'You can't go back to it at all,' he said urgently. 'If you must work, surely with your connections you can do something from home, Joss?'

'Yes. I can. But I won't earn as much money.'

'That,' he said flatly, 'is hardly a problem.'

'It is to me,' she said, eyes flashing.

'It's not a problem,' said Dan, very deliberately, 'because the solution lies in your own hands, Joss. Marry me, come and live in Kew, and work from there.'

'It sounds so cut and dried, put like that,' said Joss quietly. She looked at him intently. 'Do you really want this, Dan?'

'How many times do I have to say it? I wanted you the moment I first saw you. And I still do. But,' he added quickly, 'that needn't worry you, if you prefer a more businesslike arrangement.'

At that precise moment Joss wanted nothing more than to sink into oblivion and forget any kind of arrangement, businesslike or otherwise. She felt deeply grateful when a nurse came in to tell Dan the patient needed rest.

'I'll come to see you tomorrow,' he said, bending to kiss her cheek. 'Shall I ring Anna?'

Joss shook her head. 'No point in worrying her unnecessarily. I'll do that when I get home.' She bit her lip. 'You might ring Jack Ormond in the morning, though. Say I won't be around for a bit.'

'With the greatest pleasure,' said Dan grimly. 'Think carefully about what I said, Joss, and we'll talk about it tomorrow.'

By the time she was settled for the night Joss had made up her mind. Only a fool would turn down the chance of having the best of both worlds. If she married Dan she could still carry on with her freelancing to a certain extent, and do it in comfort, without having to worry about food and bills and all those other pressing little realities of life. Which all sounded so mercenary, she thought in distaste. Especially when she didn't really care a hang about any of it as long as she could marry Dan. And any lingering doubts disappeared next morning, when a nurse came in with a box containing a dozen yellow roses on a bed of very familiar leaves.

'Mr Armstrong rang to enquire how you are,' she said briskly. 'I'll just put these in water, then I'll have a look at you again.'

'From Dan,' said the message on the card. Joss smiled ruefully. No 'love and best wishes' from Daniel Armstrong. But the flowers were strong enough persuasion in themselves. The nurse arranged the roses against their fan of fig leaves, and when Joss was alone at last she settled back against the pillows and gazed at the perfect blooms, her hands protective on the mound moving now and then beneath the covers.

'If it's all right with you, little one,' she whispered. 'I think I'll say yes.'

CHAPTER ELEVEN

ONE brief word in the affirmative raised an instant storm of controversy about when, where, and in what style Joscelyn Georgina Hunter should be joined in marriage to Daniel Adam Francis Armstrong.

Dan, characteristically, wanted to rush her to the nearest register office the moment she said yes. Anna and her parents promptly offered Joss a reception at Glebe House, after a wedding in her father's church, while a jubilant Lord Morville urged them to both ceremony and reception at Eastlegh.

'We should have told everyone afterwards,' said Dan morosely. 'Failing that, you could at least move in with me until you decide what you do want.'

'I'm not moving to Kew until we're married,' said Joss firmly.

'Why not?'

'It fell through last time we tried it.'

'That won't happen again,' said Dan flatly.

Joss braced herself. 'Anna saw Peter Sadler the other day.'

Dan raised a hostile eyebrow. 'Did she give him the glad news?'

'Oh, yes. With great relish, she informed me.'

'Did she mention the baby?'

'Yes. That part of it didn't go down well at all.'

'No,' said Dan with grim satisfaction. 'I'm damn sure it didn't.'

They were lingering over the supper Joss had had

149

ready when Dan arrived at the flat earlier. Just like two
old marrieds, thought Joss wistfully, as they sat together
on the sofa afterwards.

'I didn't know you could cook like that,' said Dan,
stretching out his legs in comfort.

'When I'm working I don't have the time. But I first
learnt to cook with Anna's mother, when I was quite
small. She used to let us kneel up on chairs at the table
to help her.' Joss turned her head to look at him. 'Dan?'

'What's the matter?' he said instantly.

'Nothing at all.' She smiled at him. 'It's just that now
I've had time to get used to the idea I've decided how,
when and where I'd like the wedding—subject to your
approval.'

'And you want to be married in your father's church,
of course.'

'No, I don't,' she said, surprising him. 'I would miss
him too much. And though the Herricks have always
been marvellous to me I really don't feel I should put
them to the expense and bother of a reception. Not,' she
added dryly, 'that a marquee on the lawn would be necessary this time.'

Dan eyed her warily. 'Are you saying you'd prefer the
church at Eastlegh?'

'Good heavens, no! Soon enough for a wedding there
when Francis marries Sarah.' She smiled. 'Actually, I
think your idea is best. A civil ceremony first, then a
small party at your place afterwards.'

Dan looked taken aback. 'Is that what you *really*
want?'

What Joss really wanted was white silk and roses and
a choir, and a church full of people, with champagne and
witty speeches, a write-up in the *Post*'s social diary, and
a birth announcement ten months, or ten years, after-

wards. She smiled brightly and assured Dan it was exactly what she wanted.

'Then I'll get a catering firm to do the food,' he said promptly. 'How many guests were you thinking of?'

'Just the Herricks, and Anna and Hugh for me.'

'No journalists?'

'I'd rather we kept it to nearest and dearest—unless you want to invite people from your firm?'

'Not particularly.' Dan frowned, and moved closer. 'Joss, if there were no baby involved would you have preferred a bigger wedding?'

He was too quick by half. 'There wouldn't *be* a wedding without the baby,' she retorted.

'I'm hardly likely to forget!'

'I'm sorry,' she sighed. 'I didn't mean to snap.'

He gave her a dark, brooding look. 'Sometimes that tongue of yours cuts like a knife.'

So she'd actually hurt him. Joss bit her lip, her eyes filling with sudden tears, and with a stifled curse Dan closed the space between them and put his arm round her so carefully the tears turned to an unsteady chuckle.

'I won't break,' she assured him.

Dan's arm tightened a little, then his free hand reached out and touched the velvet-covered bulge for the first time. Holding her breath, Joss placed the hand over the vital spot, and Dan's entire body tensed as he stared incredulously into her eyes.

'Was that what I thought it was?'

'That's right. Miss Baby saying hello.'

'You've found out it's a girl, then?' he demanded.

'No. But it's definitely a girl. We expectant mothers know these things!' Joss looked down at the large hand, very much aware that this was the first time Dan had voluntarily touched her since they'd met up again, apart from carrying her about like a sack of potatoes.

Dan breathed in sharply as he felt kicking again, and Joss sat very still, savouring the moment of rapport. When he removed his hand at last Joss waited for him to take his arm away. But instead Dan put his hand in an inside pocket and took out a wad of tissue paper.

'This seems an appropriate time to ask if you'd like to wear this,' he said, sounding oddly unlike his normal forceful self.

'What is it?'

'Unwrap it and see.'

Joss carefully unfolded layers of tissue paper, and gazed in delight at an old-fashioned gold ring set with small diamonds interspersed with seed pearls and garnets.

Dan eyed it doubtfully. 'I could have taken you to Cartier, or whatever, but my father insisted I offer you this first.'

Joss cleared her throat. 'Was it your mother's?'

Dan nodded. 'Bought second-hand with my father's savings when they were young. If you don't care for it,' he added casually, 'we can still do the Cartier bit. No doubt Sadler gave you something more impressive.'

Joss gave him a scornful look, her heart singing as she gave him the ring. Dan must surely feel something more than just duty and responsibility to give her something so special. 'It was a small solitaire diamond—not nearly as pretty as this.' She held out her hand. 'You're supposed to put it on my finger,' she instructed, and held her breath as he slid it over her knuckle.

'I could have it made smaller,' he offered.

Joss shook her head, her eyes glued to her hand. 'No. I like it the way it is.' She looked up at him, her eyes luminous. 'It's beautiful, Dan. Is it too late to ring your father to thank him?'

'Yes,' he said firmly. 'We'll talk to him tomorrow, and tell him the plans. Maybe you can even persuade him to come up to London for the wedding.'

'But of course he must come!' said Joss, astonished.

'He doesn't like London,' Dan warned. 'He's visited me just once since I moved into the house in Kew, and even then he spent most of his time in the Gardens.'

'He'll come to the wedding,' said Joss confidently.

Now the die was cast, Joss felt better. Nothing would have made her confess it, but to refuse Dan's proposal had been the most difficult thing she'd ever done in her life. Sheer pride had forced her to say no. But from now on she could relax, prepare herself for the wedding. And if it was not the occasion of unalloyed joy it might have been in different circumstances, she was nevertheless marrying Daniel Armstrong, the father of her child. And the man she loved.

Joss obediently did her best to rest as much as possible in the time leading up to the wedding, and she was lying on her sofa with a book one morning when her doorbell rang. Her eyes lit up. Maybe Dan had called round to make sure she was following his orders. But a very different voice came over the intercom.

'Let me in, please, Joss,' said Peter Sadler urgently.

Joss stiffened. 'I will not! I'm astonished you've got the gall—'

'I've come to apologise,' he insisted. 'Talk to me just this once, Joss. *Please.*'

With reluctance Joss released the lock, and Peter ran up towards her, then stopped dead when he reached the landing, his eyes on the fall of fabric veiling her front.

'Hello, Joss,' he said, clearing his throat. His mouth twisted. 'I knew you were expecting a baby, but it's a shock just the same.'

'Hello, Peter.' She looked at him steadily for a moment, then turned and made for the sofa. 'I'm supposed to rest.'

'Anna told me you'd been in hospital,' he said, pulling out her desk chair. 'She said you'd given up your job, so I came here on the offchance of finding you in.'

'Why?' she said coldly.

'To apologise for my behaviour last time.' Colour rose in his boyish face.

'You very nearly wrecked my life,' she said without emotion.

'I was hitting out at Armstrong, not you, Joss,' he said, shamefaced.

'Just because his company turned you down!' she said incredulously.

'At the time I blamed him for everything wrong in my life. When I heard you were together it was the end. All I could think of was making him pay.'

She stared at him scornfully, then paused, frowning. 'But how on earth did you work your little scam?'

He winced. 'I'd planned it for quite a while. I conned your address from one of your pals at the *Post* beforehand. Then I came up that day, confirmed that Armstrong was in his office, and drove round here. I rang the Athena building on my carphone with the message, and waited until he was well on his way before ringing your bell. You let me in, I left your door ajar, and you know the rest.'

Joss shook her head in disbelief. 'It only worked because Dan was so frantic when he got the message he rushed straight here without ringing first.'

Peter shrugged. 'It was worth a gamble—and I won.'

She stared at him. 'So what you and I once had together meant nothing against the chance to pay Dan back for your own failure.'

His mouth twisted. 'Don't please! God, I'm sorry, Joss.' He paused. 'Besides, an apology isn't my only reason for coming.'

'Isn't it enough?' she said bitterly.

He chewed on his bottom lip, the light eyes suddenly imploring. 'Tell me the truth, Joss. Is there any chance the baby's mine?'

Joss looked at him in silence for a moment, trying to remember why she had ever thought herself in love with Peter Sadler. 'My child,' she said succinctly, 'will be born on February the fourteenth next year, give or take a day or two. You walked out in February this year. You were always a whizz with figures, Peter. Work it out.'

The following week Sam Armstrong travelled from Dorset with Francis and Sarah in the car to the house in Kew, where the three of them spent the night before the wedding with Dan.

Anna had spent a few days in Acton with Joss beforehand, looking after her like a hen with one chick, and helping in the search for a wool coat in palest creamy yellow to wear with the navy chiffon dress. Hugh and the Herricks drove up to London early on the Saturday morning to drive with them to the register office.

When Joss was in the car, holding the posy of yellow roses Dan had sent, she felt tense and apprehensive, until a sudden onset of kicking under the wickedly expensive coat reminded her that though the forthcoming ceremony was by no means compulsory, morally or any other way, she was glad Dan had insisted on a wedding. And when he came hurrying to hand her out of the car, looking magnificent in formal morning coat, her smile was so radiant he looked dazzled. Still holding Dan's hand, she reached up to kiss Sam Armstrong, who looked as magnificent as his son in formal clothes, with the addition of a fiercely stiff white collar. Then there were embraces and greetings and introductions, and half an hour later Joss was Mrs Daniel Armstrong, with marriage lines and a wide gold wedding ring to prove it. They came out to a battery of photographers from the various papers Joss worked for, and afterwards Francis and Hugh took over with their own cameras until Dan called a halt.

Dan and Joss drove back to Kew alone, leaving the rest of the party to follow behind. 'I should have hired a photographer,' he said in apology. 'Why didn't you mention it?'

'I never thought of it,' she said truthfully. 'Anyway, with Francis and Hugh snapping away, and the professional lot, we won't be short of photographs to remind us of the happy day.'

'Is it really a happy day for you?' said Dan, putting a hand on her knee.

She shot a glance at him. 'Yes. It is.'

'Then it is for me, too.' He smiled wryly. 'I wasn't sure you'd actually turn up this morning.'

Joss stared at him in astonishment. 'Were you really in any doubt?'

'Yes,' he said bluntly. 'You've been known to vanish before.'

'Not this time, Dan,' she assured him.

'You were pretty reluctant until recently. You could have changed your mind at the last minute.'

'In which case I'd have let you know, not left you waiting!'

'I kept telling myself that.' He smiled crookedly. 'But apparently brides don't hold the monopoly on wedding nerves.'

Joss laughed. '*You?* With nerves?'

'Why not? I'm human.' He glanced down at her. 'Otherwise you wouldn't be expecting my child. How is she, by the way?'

'Very lively. Must be the excitement.'

'You look very beautiful,' he said quietly, keeping his eyes on the road.

Joss gave him an oddly shy look. 'Thank you. I was so sure you'd send me yellow roses I tired Anna out in search of the coat.'

Once again his long hand, adorned now with a heavy gold ring like hers, reached out to touch Joss's knee. 'It was worth it. Motherhood seems to be adding an extra dimension to your...'

'Size?' she teased, when he paused.

'To your allure,' he said softly, in a tone which silenced her very effectively.

It was a very exuberant party which enjoyed the lunch Dan had ordered on Joss's instructions. Certain that his father would dislike picking at smart bits and pieces, Joss had ordered a conventional meal, and felt pleased when she saw Sam tucking into the salmon timbales and the roast which followed, chatting away to the Herricks as though he'd known them for years. The meal was a leisurely affair, brought to a fitting climax when a waiter brought in the wedding cake Mrs Herrick had insisted on making.

'Mother's the Annie Oakley of the icing gun,' chuckled Anna, when Sarah exclaimed on the perfection of the cake. 'She did three tiers for mine.'

'I've done two for Joss,' said Mrs Herrick, 'but I'm keeping the other one for the christening.'

There was a moment of dead silence, then Joss got up and threw her arms round Mrs Herrick and gave her a smacking kiss. 'What a lovely thought,' she said with affection, and saw Dan relax visibly before adding his own thanks.

'Come on, then, you two,' said Francis. 'Hurry up and cut the cake so I can deliver my amazingly witty speech.'

'I told him not to bother,' Dan apologised to Joss, 'but he wouldn't listen.'

'Very right and proper,' said Sam Armstrong in approval. 'It's not a wedding without speeches.'

Nor was there any lack of them. After Dan's brief speech of thanks, Francis leapt to his feet and kept everyone in gales of laughter over the combined exploits of the groom and best man in their boyhood. 'And,' he added, as the punchline, 'I insist on being godfather to the baby.'

There was a roar of applause, then Mr Herrick got up on behalf of the bride, and told Dan that though he must be congratulating himself on his lack of in-laws, he hadn't got away scot-free, since he hoped Dan would look on himself and his wife as replacements.

Then, to Dan's obvious surprise, Sam Armstrong got to his feet and raised his glass. 'It just remains for me to add my own good wishes, and ask you all to toast the happiness of my son and his lovely bride.'

At which point tears welled in the eyes of the lovely bride, and the groom efficiently whipped out a handkerchief from his pocket, having, as he informed everyone, expected this far sooner.

'It's my condition,' said Joss huskily, blowing her nose.

'A word forbidden to everyone except my wife,' warned Dan, grinning.

It was late afternoon by the time everyone bade emotional farewells, and drove off to their various destinations.

'A pity they wouldn't stay longer,' said Joss, yawning.

Dan looked down at her, lips twitching. 'You wouldn't last another ten minutes.' He held out his hands. 'Up you come.'

'Why?' she demanded.

'Time for a nap. Later on you can come down and do whatever you like for the rest of the evening, but right now you're going to rest.'

Joss knew he was right. Now everyone had gone, she felt not only tired but a little flat. 'Perhaps I will. I didn't sleep much last night.' She shrugged, smiling. 'Too excited, I suppose. And Miss Baby wasn't sleepy either, which didn't help.'

'Does she keep you awake a lot?' he asked, pulling her to her feet.

'Quite a bit.' Joss accepted Dan's hand to go upstairs. 'Where have you put my things?' she asked.

'In here.' Dan opened the door to the master bedroom. 'I'm in the room next door.'

'But I could use that,' she protested.

'You'll be more comfortable here. There's a television, and a radio, so you can stay in bed some days if you feel under the weather.'

It wasn't the first time Joss had been in Dan's rather severe bedroom. But on former occasions they'd shared the vast bed. She glanced at Dan, then away again quickly, aware that he was thinking the same thing.

'Thank you,' she said brightly.

'I've cleared out half the cupboards, but I didn't unpack your cases. I thought you'd prefer to do that yourself.' Dan showed her a buzzer on one of the bedside tables. 'This connects with my room, so if you feel ill, or you need anything, just press that.'

Secretly determined never to do any such thing, Joss wandered round the room when he was gone, picking things up and putting them down. At last she unpacked her cases and hung some of her clothes up to join the new yellow coat, put others away in drawers, then took off the beautiful chiffon dress and hung it away with the rest.

When Dan knocked on the door a couple of hours later Joss had showered, redone her face and hair and put on a comfortable brown velvet top and jersey trousers. She opened the door, smiling brightly, wondering what was required of her for their first evening as man and wife.

Dan stood leaning in the doorway, wearing a pale sweater over his favourite indigo shirt and a worn pair of navy cords.

'How do you feel?' he asked.

'Fine.'

'You look good. Are you hungry? You didn't eat much lunch.'

'I can't eat much at a time anymore. Miss Baby objects.'

'In that case how about a snack? The caterers left enough food for an army. We won't have to cook for a week.'

'We?'

'You, then,' he amended. 'I'm no expert in the kitchen.'

Since he was so amazingly expert in bed, thought Joss, going ahead of him, one couldn't have everything. Though if this marriage was to be as businesslike as he suggested, it was unlikely she'd benefit from that particular expertise unless she made it plain she wanted to. Some time.

The evening was surprisingly restful. Joss put together a light meal, and afterwards they watched a film. Later Dan insisted on making tea for her before she went to bed, then switched off the television and sat down beside her while she drank it.

'Time we had a talk,' he said firmly.

Joss looked intently at the initial on her beaker. 'What shall we talk about?'

'At this point,' he began, 'most couples would be jetting off to some exotic place for a honeymoon. We can't do that, but I've taken a few days off so we can get used to living together.'

'Are you sure you won't be bored?'

'I can honestly say that one emotion I've never experienced in your company is boredom,' he said dryly.

Joss gave him a very straight look. 'But in the past, remember, we spent a lot of time making love.'

'Do you think I'm likely to forget?' He reached out to grasp the hand adorned with the rings he'd given her. 'I think we can find pleasure in each other's company, wife, just the same. For a start, first thing Monday morning I'm taking you shopping.'

Joss chuckled. 'A dangerous plan! Anything specific?'

'Clothes and bedroom furniture for Miss Baby, for starters, a new computer for her mother, plus some walking shoes. I've been reading up on the subject, and apparently short walks are beneficial. But not in four-inch heels. So, with Kew Gardens on our doorstep we'll take a daily stroll there together, weather permitting. Do they make designer hiking shoes?' he teased.

CHAPTER TWELVE

DAN was right. Boredom played no part at all in their first week of married life together. Joss felt particularly well, the weather was good, and after the purchase of the necessary shoes their walks in Kew Gardens became a daily ritual Joss enjoyed all the more because Dan so very obviously enjoyed it too. As they walked they talked without constraint, and Dan teased her about her sudden craving for sweet things, and indulged her in cakes and cappuccinos in the tea rooms, in every way as model a husband as any new bride could wish for.

Joss felt it was unreasonable to want more. But she would have traded the extravagant accessories Dan had insisted on buying for the baby, and the expensive shoes and everything else he'd bought for his wife, in exchange for one specific word of love.

Up to this point Dan's domestic arrangements had been carried out by a cleaning firm who came in once a week, but this, he told Joss, was no longer enough. Someone was now needed on a daily basis as well.

'Is that really necessary?' Joss protested.

'If not now, it will be after the baby's born. Or would you prefer a full-time nanny?'

'Absolutely not.' Joss thought about it for a while. 'If you're going to keep the cleaning firm on perhaps we could find someone to do the daily light stuff, and look after the baby for a couple of hours while I work.'

Since Dan insisted someone must be found before his

short break was over, they consulted an agency who sent them several applicants, one of whom found instant favour with both Armstrongs.

Nan Perry was in her late thirties, married with two teenage sons, lived a bus ride away in Brentford and wanted a job with shorter hours than her present hotel work.

Joss took to the brisk, attractive young woman at once, and engaged her on the spot. And after Nan's first day Dan went back to Athena, reassured that with someone on hand who was not only sensible and pleasant, but had also been through the birth process, Joss was in good hands. But Joss missed him. Without Dan's formidable presence the house seemed empty, and she was glad to have the hard-working Nan around. Except that Nan took over tasks that Joss could well have performed herself. So with time to spare for the first time in years Joss spent some of it on familiarising herself with the new computer, and decided to write regular letters to Sam Armstrong, to involve him in the approaching arrival of his grandchild. After posting the first, she dashed off a humorous article on the joys of pregnancy, which went down so well at the *Post* she was asked to contribute in the same vein regularly until the birth, then go on afterwards to report the funny side of having a new baby.

Funny side? Joss raised a wry eyebrow, wondering just how easy it would be to write hilarious little pieces if she'd been up all night with a wailing baby.

Soon afterwards the question of Christmas arose, when pressing invitations arrived from both Warwickshire and Dorset.

'What do you want to do?' asked Dan one evening over dinner.

Joss looked thoughtful.

'Frankly I don't fancy travelling that far in either direction. Couldn't we just ask your father to come here for Christmas?'

He smiled so warmly it was obvious her answer had both surprised and delighted him. 'Are you sure?'

'Yes.' Joss smiled back, suddenly so full of love for this big, sexy, sophisticated man it was almost impossible to keep from telling him. Almost, but not quite.

'You look utterly gorgeous tonight, Mrs Armstrong,' Dan said softly.

Since she'd taken a shamelessly long time over her face and hair, Joss was glad to hear it. 'That's because I'm sitting down,' she retorted, deliberately flip. 'The illusion shatters once I'm on my feet.'

'Not for me.'

'Thank you.' Joss felt her colour rise. 'Will your father come, do you think?'

'If you ask him I'm sure he will.' Dan smiled again. 'Father isn't liberal with his affections, but as far as he's concerned you can do no wrong, Joss.'

'The feeling's mutual,' she assured him.

'It was good of you to write to him.' Dan stretched out a hand to touch hers. 'Francis rang to ask about you before I left work tonight. I gather my father's softened up so much lately he's finally consented to address His Lordship by his first name.'

'Goodness!' Joss laughed. 'As soon as we can travel after—afterwards, we'll take the baby to Eastlegh and show her off.'

Dan applied himself to his dinner, unaware that his fleeting caress had deprived his wife of her appetite until he noticed her pushing food round her plate.

'What's the matter? Not hungry tonight?'

'No, not really. I shouldn't have had tea and buns with Nan this afternoon.'

'How's she shaping?'

'Very well.' Joss grinned. 'She's got a vast list of numbers taped over the kitchen telephone, ready for the first sign of Miss Baby's birthday.'

Dan nodded approvingly. 'But when that happens I'd prefer you to ring me yourself, Joss, if you can.'

'Of course I will,' she promised, then frowned as he got up to take their plates. 'I can do that.'

He shook his head. 'I'm perfectly capable of loading a dishwasher.'

Dan Armstrong was capable of anything, reflected his wife. Except the kind of love she so desperately wanted from him.

Since Joss knew, almost to the minute, when her child had been conceived, she was sure her daughter would be born on the fourteenth, St Valentine's Day, as she'd insisted all along, and she smiled to herself as she wandered next day in Kew Gardens. Dan would never agree to calling the baby Valentine. The day was bitterly cold, and Joss pulled her knitted beret low over her eyes as she turned to make for home, wishing she hadn't walked so far. Her return was slow as she avoided patches of frost the feeble winter sun had failed to melt, and by the time she reached the house Joss was shivering, and annoyed with herself for staying out so long. When she let herself in Nan came hurrying to meet her, frowning in disapproval.

'I was just coming to look for you. You've overdone it, haven't you? Let me have your coat, then you can put your feet up on the sofa and I'll bring your tea.'

'I'd rather sit with you in the kitchen,' said Joss, in need of company. But after the tea she felt no better, and in the end gave in and let Nan help her to bed. 'I feel a bit achey,' she admitted, as Nan propped pillows behind her. 'Probably coming down with something.'

'You've caught a chill, staying out in this weather.' Nan eyed her closely. 'Shall I call the doctor?'

'Heavens, no. It's probably just a cold.' Joss smiled and snuggled down into the warmth of the bed. 'I'll have a little nap.'

When Joss woke Dan was standing over her. 'Dan? You're home early!'

'Nan rang and told me you weren't well, so I called it a day and came home.' He sat on the side of the bed and put a hand on her forehead. 'You're very hot. She said you wouldn't let her call the doctor.'

'Of course not. It was cold out and I walked too far; that's all.' She smiled, touched by the anxiety in his eyes. 'Honestly, Dan, I'm all right.'

'You don't look it,' he said shortly. 'I'll have a shower and change, then I'll bring you some tea. I told Nan to go home.'

'I'll get up and put a meal on later—'

'No, you won't.' Dan wagged a finger at her. 'You stay where you are. Nan's left some kind of casserole, so we'll have supper up here together later on. No arguments,' he added, smiling.

Joss found she had no energy to make any. She felt hot and strangely light-headed, her back ached, and the thought of staying in bed was deeply attractive. When Dan had gone off to shower she forced herself to get out of bed and make for the bathroom, then came out in utter distress, sweat beading her mouth as she pressed the buzzer. Dan burst into the room, his face as white as hers when she choked out the dreaded word 'haemorrhage.'

Dan took instant charge, rang the hospital, then carried

Joss down to the car and drove as fast as the traffic allowed, talking soothingly all the way. And shortly afterwards she was on a table in a delivery room, connected to a foetal heart rate monitor, an automatic blood pressure gauge fastened on her arm and an efficient, sympathetic nurse calming her fears as her daughter made it plain that this was no false alarm, but her birthday.

Later, at some stage in the relentless process of birth, Joss was dimly aware of Dan holding her hand in a painful grip as he mopped her sweating forehead.

'She's too early,' she sobbed, tears coursing down her cheeks, and Dan, looking haggard, raised bloodshot, questioning eyes to the nurse, who assured him that a seven-month baby was no problem.

Dan was a tower of strength, up to a point, but eventually the situation was too much for his normally iron self-control. He grew so distraught he was expelled from the room and told to come back when he was called. When he was allowed in again Joss lay exhausted and ashen pale, her hand limp and cold when he took it in both of his.

'How do you feel?' he asked hoarsely.

'Tired.' She tried to smile. 'And surprised. It's not Miss Baby after all.'

Dan smoothed back her damp hair. 'No. He's a five-pound baby boy. And in remarkably good shape in the circumstances.' His face twisted. 'Better than his mother. I was sure you were going to die.'

'So I gather. I did wonder myself at one stage. Not an uncommon reaction, I'm told.' The ghost of a smile curved her dry lips. 'Feel better now?'

He nodded wryly. 'Sorry I made a fuss.'

'Did you? I was too busy to notice.' She looked away.

'They're keeping him in a special unit but we can both leave in a week or two.'

'Surely not!' Dan frowned blackly. 'We'll see about that. I'll talk to the consultant.'

Joss looked at him anxiously. 'Have you seen the baby?'

Dan nodded. 'He's frighteningly small, but with all the necessary bits and pieces, I'm told—except a name.'

'No point in calling him Valentine now,' she murmured drowsily.

Dan stared blankly, then got up as a pair of nurses came in to send him away. 'I'll see you in the morning, Joss,' he said quickly. He hesitated for a moment, then bent to kiss her pallid cheek and said goodnight.

When Dan arrived next morning, hollow-eyed, pale, and bearing yellow roses, Joss was sitting in the special care unit, the baby in a cot beside her.

'You look like a different person,' he said with relief. 'Sorry, no fig leaves available.'

'Never mind,' she said lightly. 'The roses are lovely, thank you. Someone will deal with them later.'

When Dan returned he looked at her searchingly. 'How do you feel?'

'A bit battered and bruised in places, but otherwise not too bad.' She watched, tense, as he gazed down at the sleeping baby.

'He's bigger than I expected,' said Dan. After a long, unbearable pause he shot her a penetrating blue look. '*Is* he premature, Joss?'

She met the look head-on. 'Why not rephrase the question and say what you mean?'

Dan's face twisted. 'I have a right to know if I'm his father. Not that it makes any difference.'

Her dark-ringed eyes flashed angrily. 'Of *course* it makes a difference.'

'I meant,' he said with controlled violence, 'that his mother is my wife, so I'll claim him as my son whether I'm the father or not.'

Joss clenched her hands beneath the sheets. 'How very noble,' she said, her voice shaky with scorn. 'Or is this *claim* of yours to get in before Peter Sadler can stake his?'

'Sadler's got nothing to do with it,' he flung back.

Joss looked at him, searching. 'Do you really believe that?'

'I want to—God how I want to,' he said, suddenly weary. 'So just tell me he's not the father and I'll never mention it again.'

'Do you actually think,' she said, dangerously quiet, 'I would have married you if he were?'

Dan paused an instant too long. 'No—no, or course not.'

Joss eyed him dully. 'But you're not certain.'

Dan's eyes narrowed to blazing slits of cobalt. 'The only certainty, Joss, is that you—and the child—belong to me.'

The child, thought Joss.

Dan got to his feet, looking down at her from his great height. For all the world like a god from Olympus, surveying a frail, human mortal, she thought bitterly.

'We'll talk again tonight,' he told her.

'Have you rung your father?'

'I'll do that from my office. I wanted to wait until—'

'Until what?' she asked curiously. 'Until I confirmed whether my son is yours or not?'

Dan's jaw clenched. 'No,' he said harshly. 'I was waiting until I knew for certain that you and the baby were both in good shape.'

At least 'baby' was better than 'the child.' 'Give your father my love,' said Joss. 'He'll pass the news on to Sarah and Francis, of course. But I can ring Anna myself.'

Dan nodded, and turned to go. At the door he paused, looking back. 'Have you thought of a name? Last night you were muttering something about Valentine.'

Joss shrugged. 'Delirious, probably.'

'So what shall we call him?'

'Why, Adam, of course. Adam George.' She smiled frostily. 'I was going to put in Samuel, too. But your doubts about my son's paternity rule that out.'

Dan's mouth twisted. 'Joss, listen—'

'Could you go now, please?' she interrupted with sudden force. 'I'm tired.'

The urgency drained abruptly from his face. 'Of course.' He gazed down at the baby again, then turned on his heel and strode from the room.

In the afternoon Anna and her mother came to visit, bearing books and flowers, and a parcel of exquisite knitted garments. They crooned over the baby, and sat for a while to chat, then Mrs Herrick tactfully went ahead, leaving Anna alone with Joss.

'I called into Peter's office and told him,' she said, the moment her mother was out of earshot.

'Why?' said Joss, frowning.

'I wanted to see his face when I gave him the news.' Anna pulled a face. 'But he looked so stricken I actually felt sorry for him.'

For Joss it was a poignant, but terrifying moment to hold her baby son in her arms the day they left hospital and know that from now on she was responsible for his welfare. As she cradled the warm, wool-swathed bundle she took a deep, shaky breath, and Dan, sensing her sudden apprehension, put his arm round her and kept it there as they expressed thanks to the nursing staff gathered to see them off.

Dan helped her to install the protesting baby in the small car seat, frowning as Joss coped with unfamiliar buckles and straps. 'He's a bit small for the seat yet. Will he be safe?'

'I'll sit in the back and make sure he is,' she said, and bit her lip. 'Dan, this is so scary. Being a mother, I mean. I hope I can do it.'

Dan leaned down to look at the baby, who chose that moment to look back with an unfocused stare. 'Of course you can.' He shot a look at her as she secured her safety belt. 'He's got blue eyes.'

'All babies do,' she said matter-of-factly. Peter Sadler's eyes were also blue. Ice-blue, not dark navy. But blue.

After the return to Kew Joss found her life very quickly settled into a demanding, exhausting routine of broken nights and days of endless feeding and nappy-changing, and sometimes just walking the floor in utter panic with a baby who refused to stop crying. Nan was a tower of strength. She took over the sterilising and saw to the extra laundry, assuring Joss that everything was perfectly normal, and Adam would soon settle down. And when Joss suddenly realised that Christmas was almost on them Nan insisted on taking care of Adam for an hour or two to let Joss go shopping. Once she'd been persuaded, Joss rushed round the shops, buying presents for everyone she could think of, including Nan's boys, and ordered a Christmas tree and a turkey, and got home exhausted to find Dan home early for once, pacing the floor as he waited for her.

'Where the hell have you been?' he demanded as she came through the door, laden with parcels.

'Why? What's the matter?' she said in alarm. 'Is something wrong with Adam?'

'No. Your *son* is fine. He's with Nan. Couldn't you have spared a thought for me for a change—realised I'd worry?' he demanded, incensed, dumping packages on the hall table.

'That's not fair; you're never home at this time,' she retorted, glancing up the stairs, and with a smothered curse Dan pulled her into their sitting room and closed the door.

'What the hell were you doing, staying out so long? You look shattered.'

'I've been shopping,' she flung at him. 'For the first time since Adam arrived. I was out buying Christmas presents—with my own money, at that.'

He seized her by the shoulders, his eyes furious. 'Do you think I care how much money you spend? I was *worried*, woman.'

Joss could cope with his anger, but his solicitude brought tears she couldn't control, and with a sharp intake of breath Dan pulled her close and rubbed his cheek against her hair.

'Don't cry, Joss. Please.' He turned her face up to his, then took a handkerchief from his breast pocket and mopped her face. 'Look. We can't go on like this. I'm your husband, for better or worse, so for God's sake let's be friends, if nothing else.'

Joss sniffed inelegantly, conscious that she'd had no attention to spare for Dan, or anything else, since Adam's arrival. Even their dinners together rarely went undisturbed by protests from the baby listener. And her broken nights were spent in the master bedroom, alone with her son.

'You're right, Dan. As usual.' She took the handkerchief from him and scrubbed at her eyes. 'Sorry to howl like Adam—' She stopped, met his eyes and began to laugh. 'And can he howl!'

Dan chuckled, his relief undisguised for once. 'Let's make a deal,' he suggested. 'If I come home early in future I'll tell you in advance.'

'Done,' said Joss, then said impulsively, 'I think you should come home early more often.'

His eyes gleamed in response. 'Then I will, Mrs Armstrong.' He bent and kissed her with such tenderness Joss had to fight to control another rush of tears. 'Come on. I'll give you a hand with Adam's bathtime.'

Joss's first Christmas as Dan's wife and Adam's mother passed in an exhausted, but oddly happy blur, and in some strange way cemented her relationship with Dan far more firmly than a less hectic kind of Christmas could have done. Sam Armstrong arrived a few days beforehand, and, far from being an extra burden, as Dan had expected, proved to be a godsend. Nan was given the week off, to spend with her family, but Joss hardly had time to miss her because Sam was always ready to hold the baby, or peel vegetables, or make cups of tea, and even, to Dan's astonishment, wheel the baby out in his pram in Kew Gardens when it was fine, so that an exhausted Joss could have a nap.

When Sam left after New Year she begged him to come back again whenever he could.

'Dan can drive you down to Eastlegh as soon as you feel up to it, my dear,' he said gruffly, and surprised his son by folding Joss, baby and all, into a loving embrace before Dan drove him to the station.

Joss waved them off with a wry little smile. Whatever doubts Dan might still harbour about Adam, Sam Armstrong had none at all.

'He looks just like you did as a baby,' he'd told Dan. 'Same eyes as me.'

Joss gradually grew less nervous about looking after Adam, but life still kept to a relentless pattern of broken nights and exhausting days. Then one night he slept the entire night through, and Joss gave a little scream of alarm next morning, and leapt out of bed to rush to the cot.

'What is it?' said Dan, as he catapulted, half-naked, into the room.

'Adam slept all night,' said Joss, and giggled, feeling utterly silly. 'Sorry to startle you.'

Dan grinned, and wagged a finger at the stirring baby. 'You scared the hell out of your mother, young man. And me. But a good night's sleep is a great idea. Try another one tonight.'

Joss hesitated. 'Are you in a hurry?'

'Why?'

'I'd love a shower before I get Adam up. Could you watch him for a few minutes?'

Dan raised an eyebrow. 'You mean you trust me with your cub, Madam Tigress?'

Joss coloured, well aware that it was an effort to trust her son to anyone. Even Dan. 'Yes, of course. I won't be long.'

When she rushed back, breathless, with her damp hair bundled up in a knot, Dan was standing at the window with the baby in his arms. He turned, grinning. 'If they ever make showering an Olympic discipline you'll win a gold medal.'

'I didn't want to hold you up,' she panted, and held out her arms.

But Dan lifted the baby high in the air, triumphant as Adam gave an unmistakable crow of approval. 'You like that? Good. We'll try it again later. But right now your mother wants you back.' He handed the baby over. 'Let Nan look after him more. She's all for it, Joss, and it won't do Adam any harm.'

Joss knew he was right. Her articles on *Life with Baby* were all written at odd moments, whenever Adam deigned to sleep. Whereas Nan, she knew, would happily wheel the baby in the park and give Joss a regular space to herself, for writing or researching, or just doing nothing. It was the reason, Joss reminded herself, why Nan had been engaged in the first place.

Adam was three months old before Joss could bring herself to let him sleep in his bedroom. She put the baby listener beside her bed, but the first night she woke every hour during the night to check on him, and just as dawn was breaking collided with Dan outside his room.

'Go back to bed,' he whispered. 'He's fine. I've just covered him up.'

Reluctantly Joss got back into the vast, lonely bed, and tried to sleep, but a few minutes later shot upright again as Dan came in.

'What's the matter?' she asked in fright, throwing back the covers.

Dan put a mug of tea on the bedside table and thrust her back again. 'Nothing's the matter. I just want you to drink that tea and sleep for a while.' He picked up the small monitor. 'I'm taking this. If Adam wakes I'll see to him until I'm ready to leave.'

Spring was showering Kew Gardens with blossom when Dan decided he could leave Athena and all its demands to his staff for a while and take a holiday.

'Time we went down to Eastleigh,' he announced.

Joss was all for it, and felt as though life was beginning to fall into place at last. Adam had sailed through his three-month check-up that morning. She had completed an article well before deadline that afternoon, while Nan had walked him in the Gardens, and even had time for a leisurely bath before they returned. Once her son was tucked up in his cot Joss had changed into a new pink sweater and black velvet jeans only one size larger than her pre-Adam days, and from the sudden leap of heat in Dan's eyes when he arrived home she knew she looked a lot more like the Eve he'd once desired so fiercely.

'I'd like that,' said Joss, pouring coffee. 'When shall we go?'

'As soon as you like.' Dan relaxed in his chair, contemplating her with approval. 'You look better these days, Joss.'

'I feel better.' She handed him his cup, smiling. 'A few hours' sleep occasionally make a world of difference.'

'I'll tell my father we'll travel down this weekend.' Dan paused. 'We could probably stay at Home Farm if you think the cottage might be a tight fit.'

'Certainly not!' said Joss indignantly. 'We stay with your father or we don't go.'

'Pax!' he said, holding up a hand. 'I was only thinking of you, Joss. As usual,' he added deliberately.

Joss flushed and looked away, and a moment later Dan got up to switch on the television for the news. She stared at the screen, wondering if her husband would ever suggest joining her in his own vast bed. If he only knew it, she longed to bridge the gap between them. It refused to heal completely because Dan, she was sure, still harboured doubts about Adam's pedigree. But if he did he never let them stand in the way between him and the baby. Adam was fast growing from the amorphous baby stage into a little person, who chuckled fatly when Dan swung him up in the air or nuzzled the moist, irresistible skin of Adam's neck. Adam responded joyfully to this large, exciting male person, who played with him far too roughly sometimes for Joss's liking. But she never said so, only too pleased to encourage any contact between the two loves of her life. And some day soon, Joss knew, she would just have to talk to Dan about the doubts and passions simmering beneath the surface of their new relationship. When they returned from Eastlegh, perhaps.

By the time they were ready to leave for Dorset the car was so crammed with necessities for Adam that Dan told Joss a second car would be necessary if she came up with another thing. 'And I demand your company on the journey,' he said firmly, 'so leave everything else behind and get in the car!'

Their welcome at Eastlegh was warm. Sam Armstrong gave Joss a swift kiss, wrung his son's hand, then reached into the back to take Adam from his car seat. For a moment the baby regarded this male person with suspicion, then his face creased into a smile, and Sam, delighted, bore him proudly into the house.

'You'd better give Home Farm a ring,' he told Dan. 'I promised I'd let them know when you arrived.'

Soon there was a noisy reunion with Francis and Sarah, with much fuss made over the baby, who lapped up the attention in a way which amused Francis enormously.

'Look at him. Cock of the walk, just like his father.

Poor lad,' he said, shaking his head. 'A beautiful mother like Joss, but he's saddled with his father's looks.'

'Francis!' cried Sarah. 'Don't be rude. You're right, though; he's the image of his daddy. Look at those eyes! But he's gorgeous just the same—aren't you, my darling? Can I hold him, Joss?'

By the time tea had been drunk and Sarah had been coaxed into relinquishing the baby it was time for Adam's bath.

'I'll see to that,' said Dan quickly, and smiled at Joss. 'I've put the gadgets in the kitchen, and the rest is upstairs. You can sort things out while I scrub this chap.'

Francis and Sarah took reluctant leave, after extracting a promise from Joss to come over later with Dan for coffee and a drink after dinner.

'Grandpa will babysit,' said Sarah, smiling at Sam.

Joss looked doubtful. 'I don't think—'

'You go out for an hour, my girl,' said Sam firmly. 'I'll look after him. And if I can't manage I'll ring Home Farm and you can be back here in two minutes.'

'Do you good,' said Dan, and smiled wryly at the others. 'I haven't been able to persuade my wife outside the door since Adam was born.'

Joss flushed, laughing. 'I never realised motherhood was such a full-time job.'

'What you really mean,' said Dan deliberately, 'is that you're so much in love with your son you can't bear to tear yourself away from him.'

Francis put a friendly arm round Joss. 'Do come. Just for an hour. Adam's grandfather knows all about little boys, I assure you.'

Aware that Dan was eyeing them coldly, Joss detached herself, smiling. 'Right. We'll come.'

'Armed with cellphone,' said Dan dryly, and hoisted the baby higher. 'See you later.'

When Joss went upstairs she discovered what Dan had meant by a tight fit for visitors. There was one bathroom, and two bedrooms, one of which would be shared by two adults and a baby in a Moses basket.

Because his grandfather had come to watch, Adam's bathtime was not only a noisy, protracted affair, but it tired Adam out. After despatching his supper with voracious appetite the baby fell asleep in his mother's arms and settled down without a murmur in the strange bedroom.

'Wonderful!' said Dan as they began on their meal. 'It's rare that Joss and I enjoy dinner uninterrupted.'

'Well, you can tonight,' said Sam firmly, and gestured at the baby listener. 'The young rascal's snoring, so you eat up, Joscelyn, while you've got the chance.'

Adam was still fast asleep when Dan finally persuaded Joss to leave. 'He'll be fine,' he assured her as they drove over to Home Farm.

'I know.' Joss smiled guiltily. 'I never dreamed I'd be such a doting mother.'

It was very pleasant to spend an evening with Sarah and Francis, knowing that the baby was in good hands. Joss listened, relaxed, to their wedding plans, and drank an unaccustomed glass of wine, laughing as Francis began talking about the scrapes he'd used to get into with Dan. And it was Dan, in the end, who pointed out that although no call had come from their babysitter it was time to go.

'You enjoyed that,' he said, as they drove back to the cottage.

'Yes,' said Joss, yawning. 'I did. I hope Adam hasn't worn your father out.'

'It would take more than one small baby to do that,' Dan assured her, chuckling.

And he was right. When they got back Joss was astonished to find that, although Adam had woken up at ten, Sam Armstrong had coped admirably.

'I warmed up one of those bottles you left,' he said smugly. 'Then I changed him, fed him and put him back. He's fast asleep again.'

Joss exchanged a look with her highly amused husband, then gave Sam an affectionate hug. 'Thank you. You're wonderful.'

'Nonsense,' he said gruffly. 'Now you two get off to bed and get some rest while you can. And don't worry if the lad wakes in the night. I won't mind.'

Once they'd witnessed the sleeping miracle with their own eyes, Dan smiled at Joss in apology. 'I meant to give you time to yourself to get ready for bed, but old habits die hard,' he whispered. 'When my father says jump, I still jump.'

'Does he realise how unique he is in that?' queried Joss, taking off her earrings.

'Actually, he's not,' said Dan, looking down at her. 'I feel the same about you.'

She stared at him, her heart thumping. 'I seriously doubt that!'

'It's true,' he said casually, and made for the door. 'I'll use the bathroom first.'

Later, listening to snuffling baby noises from the crib beside her, Joss lay determinedly still in the darkness which was so much more intense here in the depths of the country than in London. Dan lay equally quiet beside her. And from his very stillness Joss knew that he was just as conscious of their proximity as she was. But for the entire time they spent at Eastlegh Dan scrupulously avoided any physical contact in bed, except by accident when he was asleep. Even Daniel Armstrong, thought his wife, couldn't control the odd touch when he was unconscious.

When they returned to London Dan decided to take a few more days off. 'I should spend more time with my family,' he announced, after everything was unloaded from the car. 'I'll start by giving Adam his bath while you stack his gear away. And later,' he added, as he started upstairs with the baby, 'perhaps we can achieve a peaceful meal together for once.'

Sam had sent them home laden with fresh vegetables and new-laid eggs, and after Adam was settled down for the night Joss made Spanish omelettes for supper. Dan insisted on opening a bottle of smooth red wine, but they ate in the kitchen rather than use up valuable time by laying the dining table.

'Who knows how long our son will leave us in peace?' said Dan, very deliberately.

Our son, thought Joss, and applied herself to her omelette with sudden appetite. 'Perhaps your father has sorted him out for us.'

The evening was a vivid contrast to some of those they'd tried to spend together since Adam's birth. The baby slept until ten, then woke to demand his supper, but afterwards he went down again with a promptness Joss found hard to trust.

'Will you listen for him while I have a bath?' she asked when she rejoined Dan.

He smiled at her over his paper. 'Of course. Take your time.'

Joss took him at his word. Reading in the bath was a luxury since Adam's advent, and she stretched out in hot, scented water with a sigh of pleasure, determined to concentrate on her novel rather than ponder over whether Dan really believed, at last, that Adam was his son.

She succeeded so well the water got cold, and Joss jumped out hastily, guilty at having taken so long. She dried herself hurriedly, brushed her teeth and slapped on some moisturiser, then pulled a thin pink lawn nightgown over her head and hurried into the bedroom, to find her husband sitting propped against the pillows of his vast bed, apparently absorbed in a book.

Joss stood motionless, her heart beating like a drum as Dan looked up.

'Before you ask, he's fast asleep,' he informed her, and turned down the covers beside him. 'We shared a bed so amicably at the cottage I thought we should carry on.' His eyes met hers. 'It doesn't commit you to anything.'

Without a word, Joss crossed the room and slid into bed beside Dan. He reached out an arm, switched off the lamp, then lay in silence for so long that Joss was rigid with tension by the time he turned towards her. 'This seems the right time, at last, to ask if you'll forgive me, Joss.'

'For what, in particular?' she whispered, breathing in his familiar male scent.

'For doubting that Adam was my son, for a start. Not that it would matter if he wasn't. He's mine now.'

'He always was.'

'I know.' Dan felt for her hand and held it tightly. 'Down at Eastlegh it was suddenly easy to sort out my priorities. You, darling, are all I want. All I've ever wanted from the moment I first saw you. But because I'm a jealous fool I asked a stupid question that day in the hospital and risked losing you. And losing Adam with you.'

Joss lay very still, her entire body irradiated with heat

from his touch. 'I wouldn't have left you. I married you, Dan.'

His grasp tightened. 'If you'd wanted to go I knew damn well a few lines on a piece of paper wouldn't have kept you with me.'

'True.'

'So why did you stay?'

'Isn't it obvious?'

He pulled on her hand gently, drawing her closer. 'Are you, by any wonderful, unbelievable chance, saying you love me perhaps even a fraction as much as I love you?'

Joss fought to control her sudden trembling. This was no moment to go to pieces.

Dan waited a moment, then took her in his arms. 'If you don't love me yet I'm going to spend the rest of my life teaching you how,' he said, to her amazement, and kissed her with sudden, uncontrolled desperation. 'Do you know,' he said in her ear, his breath scorching her skin, 'how hard it was to lie with you in bed at the cottage and not touch you?'

'Yes.'

'Was it so obvious?'

'No. But I felt the same.'

Dan gave a great, relishing sigh of satisfaction, and began to kiss her in the way she had missed and longed for so desperately. His kisses were light and tender at first, but the tenderness gradually changed to a demand she answered fiercely. She shivered in delight as her body thrilled to his touch, and at last let herself gasp out her love against his lips. For a split second Dan was still, then he crushed her in a rib-cracking embrace and said a great many things which filled her with joy as he began a renewed seduction of her senses, every touch adding fuel to the fire that flamed between them at such overwhelming speed neither of them had any resistance against the bright, burning magic which consumed them in a fever of sensation so intense it was almost pain.

Long afterwards, when they had achieved something like calm, Dan raised his head slightly. 'Will you repeat that in cold blood, Mrs Armstrong?'

'My blood's not very cold yet,' she panted, 'but I'll happily repeat that I love you as often as you want. Now.'

'Why now?' he demanded.

'Now you've admitted you love *me*, of course.'

He reached out an arm and switched on the light. 'But I've told you that all along,' he said, frowning down into her flushed face.

'No,' she corrected. 'You told me you wanted me. There's a difference.'

Dan stared at her in blank astonishment. 'You mean that my choice of vocabulary was the barrier between us all this time?'

Joss shook her head. 'No. The big obstacle was your doubt about your son's pedigree.'

Dan leaned his forehead against hers. 'So if I still harboured these doubts—which I never have, in my heart of hearts—what we just shared would never have happened?'

Joss gave him a swift kiss. 'Possibly.' She leaned over to reach into her bedside drawer. 'But because you did lay claim to my baby in the end I'll give you a reward.'

'A reward?' he repeated huskily, his fingertip tracing a pattern on her bare back. 'Can I choose the reward I want?'

'I think you'll like this one,' said Joss, and handed him an envelope.

Dan's eyes narrowed incredulously as he took out a card from Peter Sadler.

'*Congratulations on the birth of your son. Arithmetic was always my strongest point,*' said the message.

Dan raised a questioning eyebrow, 'Arithmetic?'

Joss touched a hand to his face. 'If I explain will you promise not to lose your temper and storm off into the other room?'

'I'll promise the last bit,' he said, his eyes softening. 'From now on we sleep together, my darling.'

'Good.' Joss smiled at him luminously, then told him about Peter Sadler's second visit before the wedding, how he'd planned the scene Dan had walked in on purely as a means to get back at the man behind Athena.

'He did that out of petty revenge?' said Dan in outrage. 'If I'd been there I'd have rearranged his pretty little face.'

'He didn't really come to apologise. That was an excuse. He wanted to know if he was the father of my baby,' said Joss baldly.

Dan looked at her for a moment, then drew her back into his arms and smoothed her head against his shoulder. 'And you kicked him out?'

'I did better than that. I told him the baby was due on February the fourteenth.'

Dan was suddenly still. 'When did Sadler walk out on you?'

'February last year. Which is why he put the bit about arithmetic on the card.'

'So,' said Dan slowly, 'even if Adam were a full-term baby there was never any question about who was his father.'

'No.' Joss raised her head to look up into Dan's eyes, and found him looking down at her with a strange, wry expression. 'What is it?'

'Why didn't you tell me this before?'

'I objected to the idea of producing evidence that Adam was your son. This is marriage, Daniel Armstrong, not a court of law.' Joss looked at him steadily. 'I wanted you to take him—and me—on trust.'

'As I should have done,' he said heavily. 'Not that there was ever any question about the taking and keeping. But I own to one fleeting, human second of doubt. Can you forgive me for that, my darling?' he asked, in a tone which brought her face up to his for a kiss of passionate absolution. Dan caught her close and kissed her back, then they both shook with laughter as an imperious cry came through the speaker by the bed. Dan threw back the covers and pulled on a dressing gown.

'Stay where you are. I'll see to him.'

Joss looked at him uncertainly. 'Are you sure?'

'Of course I am. It's time Adam started sleeping through anyway. I'll mention it to him when I put him down.' Dan turned in the doorway, smiling. 'But don't go away. I'm coming back.'

Joss stretched luxuriously. 'When you do, perhaps we can talk about rewards again.'

'We will. And this time I'll have what *I* want,' said Dan firmly, his eyes gleaming. 'Want to guess what it is?'

'Do *I* get a reward if I'm right?'

'Anything you want, my darling.'

'I want exactly the same as you,' she said demurely, then fended him off, laughing, as he dived across the room to kiss her. 'Hurry up, your son's getting furious in there.'

'My son will just have to wait a minute while I kiss his mother,' said Dan against her lips. 'It took me far too long to get *my* priorities right. Adam can start learning about his right now.'